THE CREEP'S AT IT AGAIN

THE CREEP'S AT IT AGAIN

Janet Adele Bloss

Illustrated by Don Robison

For my husband, Ron

Published by Willowisp Press, Inc.
401 E. Wilson Bridge Road, Worthington, Ohio 43085

Printed in the United States of America

10 9 8 7 6 5 4 3 2 1

ISBN 0-87406-345-0

One

JESSE Andrews hugged her books as she walked home from school with her best girlfriends, Karen and Biff. She just couldn't stop thinking about what had happened in school that day.

"Just think!" Jesse sighed. "Me, Jesse Andrews, in a TV commercial. Everyone will see me on television. I'll be famous all over town! Maybe even all over the country!"

"What about me!" exclaimed Biff. "Maybe Mr. Peters will choose me for the commercial. I'll bet he wants a girl with long hair." Biff's dark hair flowed loosely down her back. Now that she was twelve, she felt that she was too old for braids.

"Have you ever noticed that kids in TV commercials always have freckles?" asked Karen. A cluster of tan speckles covered her nose. "Maybe Mr. Peters will choose *me*." Karen's eyes sparkled in hope.

Jesse smiled at her two best friends. The three girls had shared everything over the years. They shared lunches at school and clothes on the weekends. They shared the good things and the bad things. Now they shared the hope of becoming the lucky kid to appear in a television commercial.

"I talked with Veronica Peters at school today," said Jesse. "I think she likes me. Maybe she'll tell her dad to pick me."

"It must be neat to have a father who's a television producer," said Biff.

"Can I be on TV, too?" a small voice piped up.

Jesse rolled her eyes at the sound of her little brother Mikey's voice. Mikey pushed his way between the girls. Then he whirled around on the sidewalk ahead of them. "I'm a TV star!" he shouted. "I'm Superman!"

"Super Creep is more like it," muttered Jesse.

Biff and Karen smiled. "He's not so bad," said Karen. "My little sister Kimmy is just as silly as Mikey."

"Can I be on TV, too?" asked Mikey again.

"Can-I-can-I-can-I?" He looked up excitedly at Jesse with big brown eyes. Then he balanced his Mickey Mouse lunch box on his head. "I can do tricks!" he exclaimed. "See?"

The lunch box fell to the ground with a clatter. The lid flew open and half of a bologna sandwich slid across the sidewalk. Jesse heaved a deep sigh. "No, Mikey," she said. "They want older kids to do the commercials. Veronica says her dad wants someone from the sixth grade."

"I am in sixth grade," Mikey protested. "I'm six years old."

"It's not the same thing," said Jesse. "Just because you're six years old doesn't mean that you're in sixth grade."

Mikey's face fell into a frown. Then a smile tugged at the corners of his lips. "Can I be on TV if Mr. Bump comes with me?" he asked. "Mr. Bump is the best actor in the world!"

Karen covered a giggle behind her hand.

"Mr. Bump is a frog," said Jesse in a quiet but tense voice. "How can a smelly old frog be an actor?"

"He went to Frog Acting School," persisted Mikey. "He learned how to be in commercials. Hey, don't walk so fast!"

Mikey's short legs hurried to catch up with the older girls. The three girls stopped at a street corner. Biff and Karen said goodbye and headed down Elm Street. Jesse and Mikey turned onto Robinwood Lane. Jesse saw their little white house in the distance. Her mother's blue car was in the driveway.

Mikey dashed in front of Jesse. She watched him as he ran across the Andrews' yard and disappeared through the side door. *He's impossible,* Jesse thought to herself as she followed him into the house.

Jesse was just in time to see her mom take a pan of brownies from the oven and set it on the table to cool. Jesse's mom caught Mikey's hand as he reached for the pan.

"Careful!" she warned. "You'll burn yourself. These brownies are for *after* dinner."

Jesse removed her jacket while Mikey ran to his room to change out of his school clothes. Moments later he reappeared, holding a big brown frog. Mikey petted the frog's cold, bumpy head. "Don't worry, Mr. Bump," he said. "You can be on TV, too. We'll both be famous!"

"Mom, you won't believe it," Jesse explained to her mom in a rush of words. "Veronica Peters is a new girl in my class at school. Her father makes commercials for TV. He wants a kid in our class to be in one of his commercials. Tryouts are next Thursday in the gym after school. Is it okay if I stay late after school next Thursday? I won't be able to walk Mikey home. Could you pick up Mikey when you get off from work?"

"Wait, slow down!" Jesse's mother said with a smile. Then a worry line ran across her forehead. "Oh, dear," she said. "Next week is when I start staying late at work. We just got a new shipment of dresses in. They have to be tagged."

"But, Mom . . ." Jesse began.

"It's just for one month, Jesse. Just for November," Mrs. Andrews continued. "Could you try out for the commercial next month?"

"No-o-o," Jesse moaned. "Next Thursday is the only time we can try out."

"I'm sorry, Jesse," said Mrs. Andrews. "But Mikey can't walk home from school by himself. Someone has to take care of him until I get home."

Jesse sighed. *It's not fair!* she thought to herself. *Mikey always ruins everything!*

Jesse heard the front door open.

"Daddy's home!" yelled Mikey.

10

Mr. Andrews walked into the kitchen. Sniffing the air, he said, "M-m-m-m-m. Smells good in here. Brownies?" Jesse looked up at her father's smiling face. Maybe he would have an answer to her problem. Maybe he would understand how much she wanted to be a television star.

The first thing Mr. Andrews said after he heard the whole story was, "Well, Stardoodle." Jesse loved it when her dad called her by her nickname. Her father called her "Stardoodle" and called Mikey "Winkypopper."

"Well, Stardoodle," Mr. Andrews repeated. "What if you take Mikey with you? He can behave for an hour or two during the tryouts. Okay?"

"Yippee!" yelled Mikey. "I'm going to be a TV star with Jesse! Mr. Bump can come with us!" He held Mr. Bump high over his head. The frog's long legs kicked at the air.

"But Mr. Peters might not want little kids around," Jesse said pleadingly. "Can't you get a baby-sitter for Mikey? Just for one day?"

"I'm sure Mr. Peters can handle one more child in the gymnasium," said Mrs. Andrews.

Yeah, Jessie thought to herself, *but having Mikey along is like having ten extra kids in the gym. Ten extra wild kids.*

"When you have your tryout, we'll help you," said Mikey. "Look! Mr. Bump can dance."

Mikey held the frog and moved him up and down. Mr. Bump's webbed feet brushed back and forth across the tabletop.

Jesse sat at the kitchen table. She leaned her head onto the palm of her hand and groaned.

"Look," continued Mikey. "Mr. Bump is doing a TV commercial for frog food."

Mikey set Mr. Bump on the table. Then he began speaking in a squeaky voice, pretending to be Mr. Bump. "Hello, boys and girls," he said. "I'm Mr. Bump. I love frog food. You'll love frog food, too. If you eat it, you'll turn into a *frog*!"

Mikey began giggling. "Everyone who eats it will be a frog!" he exclaimed. "Jesse will eat it and she'll be a giant frog. She'll hop all the way to school. She'll have extra-big feet. And she can't wear any shoes when she's a frog."

Mikey doubled over with laughter. Jesse just rolled her eyes and said, "Promise me one thing, Mikey—that you'll be quiet during tryouts in the gym. Okay?"

"Wait until Mr. Peters sees Mr. Bump!" Mikey went on. "He'll love him! He'll want him to be in *all* the commercials! Mr. Bump and I will help you, Jesse. Don't worry!"

Jesse rested her head on the table again, plenty worried. She covered her head with her hands. "Rats!" she muttered to herself. "Why does Mikey have to ruin everything?"

Mrs. Andrews patted Jesse's shoulder. "He's just a little boy," she said. "What harm can he do?"

"I'm afraid to find out," sighed Jesse. "Oh, gross! Look! The frog's in the brownies!"

Sure enough, Mr. Bump had hopped across the table and into the brownie pan. Streaks of chocolate frosting covered his legs and his webbed feet.

Mikey grinned. "He's practicing a brownie commercial. He'll be ready for Jesse's tryouts."

Mr. Andrews grabbed Mr. Bump. "Mikey, I think the kitchen is no place for frogs."

It's also no place for little brothers, Jesse thought to herself. *At least not when a brother is as creepy as mine is. I'll bet anything that my brother is the biggest creep in the world.*

"Can we eat the brownies now?" asked Mikey.

"Oh, gross!" Jesse said loudly and left the kitchen with a sigh.

Two

WHEN Jesse arrived at school the next day, she found that the entire sixth grade class at Emory Elementary and Middle School was excited and nervous about the TV commercial tryouts. All the kids she passed in the halls were talking about it.

At lunch, Jesse carried her tray through the cafeteria, walking with Biff and Karen. Looking around, she saw a familiar head of red, curly hair. "Look!" she exclaimed to her friends. "There's Veronica Peters, over there. Let's sit by her."

Jesse led the way, and Biff and Karen followed her to Veronica's lunch table. As they set their trays down, Veronica looked up in surprise.

"Hi," said Jesse. "Remember me?"

"Sure, I remember you," Veronica said. "Are you going to come to the commercial tryouts next week?"

"You bet I am!" Jesse said.

"Me, too!" Biff said.

"Same here!" Karen echoed, with a toss of her head.

Veronica shrugged her shoulders. "I think *everyone* in the sixth grade is trying out," she said. "Girls *and* boys. It'll probably take all week for Dad to choose someone.

"You know," Veronica continued, smiling, "the last person who was in one of Dad's commercials got a part in a movie. A director saw her in the commercial and thought she was cute. Next thing you know, a Hollywood director put her in a movie."

"Gee," sighed Jesse. "That's neat!"

Jesse looked across the table at Veronica Peters. Veronica sure was pretty with her red, curly hair and clear, blue eyes. Her clothes were really neat, too. Just think! Her father made TV commercials! He probably knew famous people! Veronica must have the most exciting life in the world.

"What kind of kid is your father looking for?" Jesse asked Veronica. "Does he want someone with a nice smile?" Jesse leaned across the table, grinning from ear to ear.

Suddenly Biff and Karen began to giggle. "You've got spinach stuck between your teeth," Biff said.

Jesse closed her mouth quickly. Then she rubbed her teeth with her finger.

"I don't know what kind of kid Dad wants," said Veronica. "He hasn't told me anything about this commercial."

The bell rang, and lunchtime was over. The four girls returned their trays to the kitchen and joined the crowd leaving the cafeteria. Jesse found herself walking beside Veronica.

"Your dad sounds really neat," Jesse said. "It must be exciting to have a dad who knows all kinds of TV stars."

Veronica nodded her head. "It is," she said. "He's the best. He's won all kinds of awards and trophies. He has a room full of them." Veronica looked thoughtful. Then she said, "Would you like to come over after school today? I can show you some of Dad's awards. You can see pictures of him with movie stars. Maybe he'll even be home and you can meet him."

"Wow!" Jesse exclaimed. "That would be great! I've never met a TV director before."

☆　☆　☆　☆　☆

After school, Jesse stood by the front door of Emory Elementary and Middle School. Mikey waited impatiently beside her. "Where are Biff and Karen?" he asked.

"I told them to go ahead," Jesse said. "We're not walking home together."

"Where are we going?" asked Mikey. He poked a finger into his nose and twisted it around.

"Stop it!" ordered Jesse. "Mikey, please don't do things like that in front of Veronica. It's embarrassing."

"Is Veronica the movie star girl?" Mikey asked.

Jesse sighed. "She's not a movie star. Her father makes commercials for television. Here she comes! Now behave!"

Veronica appeared, holding a stack of books under her arm. She looked from Jesse down to Mikey. "Who's that?" she asked.

"That's my little brother," said Jesse apologetically. "I have to take care of him after school. But it's only for one month," she added hurriedly.

Mikey looked up curiously at Veronica. "Can I be on TV, too?" he asked. "I could ride a motor-

17

cycle. Or I could fight a monster."

"Mikey!" Jesse said impatiently. "You're too young. I already told you that."

Jesse and Veronica walked away from the school with Mikey in between them. "Look!" he said. "I can fly!"

Mikey flapped his arms by his sides and ran ahead of the girls, zigzagging across the sidewalk. "Weeee-ooooooo Weeee-oooooo!" he shrieked. "I'm an airplane. Weeee-oooooooo!"

Jesse felt her ears go warm. Warm ears always meant that she was embarrassed. She glanced at Veronica. "Sorry," she said. "Little brothers can be a pain."

Veronica didn't say a word. She just stared at Mikey doing his airplane imitation. Then Mikey ran back to the girls. Huffing and puffing, he slowed to a walk. Between breaths, he said, "I can do a somersault. Want to see me?"

"No, thank you," Veronica said.

Jesse grabbed the back of Mikey's jacket. "You can't do a somersault on the sidewalk," she said. "It's too hard on your head."

"I bet Superman could do it," said Mikey. "I bet he could pick this sidewalk up and throw it to the moon. I bet he could kick this sidewalk to pieces if he wanted to."

Jesse put her hand over Mikey's mouth. She held it there a moment while Mikey tried to talk. Then suddenly she yelled, "Gross!" She snatched her hand away and rubbed it against the side of her coat. "You licked my hand!" she said, wrinkling her nose. "Gross!"

Mikey fell into a giggling fit. "I'm a dog!" he said. He stuck his tongue out and licked the air.

Veronica turned to Jesse. "Does your brother have some kind of problem?" she asked. "So far he thinks he's an airplane, Superman, and a dog."

"I know he's weird," Jesse admitted. "He's showing off because he wants to be in the TV commercial. Just try to ignore him."

Jesse and Mikey followed Veronica into her front yard. Jesse looked at the the large, gray stone house. She had never seen anything like it. It was at least three stories high. Big, white pillars framed the front door. Jesse could see a tennis court off to the side.

"Wow," murmured Jesse. "Pretty house."

They walked up to the porch and entered the front door. Veronica led them down a dark hallway.

"Veronica! Is that you?" A voice came from

somewhere in the back of the house.

"It's me, Mom," Veronica shouted back. "Is Dad home?"

Jesse heard footsteps and then a woman she figured was Mrs. Peters appeared, wearing a shiny blue dress. Her jewel earrings glittered. "He flew to Hollywood, darling. He'll be back tomorrow."

"Is he making a movie about frogs?" asked Mikey. "Can Mr. Bump be in it?"

Mrs. Peters smiled. She bent lower and gently squeezed Mikey's chin. Those diamond earrings flashed like stars. "What a cute little boy," she said.

Jesse was glad that at least Mrs. Peters liked Mikey. Why was it that grown-ups always thought he was so cute? After all, what was cute about a little boy who picked his nose and sometimes forgot to flush the toilet? And what was cute about a little boy whose best friend was a big, ugly, brown frog?

"I want to show Jesse some of Dad's trophies," said Veronica.

"That's fine, darling," Mrs. Peters said. "Just don't touch any of the cameras in Daddy's library. Okay?"

Mrs. Peters headed back down the hallway. Veronica led Jesse and Mikey into a room that looked like a library. Shelves of books lined one wall. The other walls were covered with photographs and awards. One award said:

TO MR. CALVIN PETERS
FOR EXCELLENCE IN THE FIELD OF
COMMERCIAL ART

Jesse looked more closely at the photographs. One was a picture of a beautiful blond woman in a silver dress. Her lipstick was dark red. Scrawled across the photo were the words:

To Calvin, my dear, dear friend who gave me my start in movies. I'll never forget you!
Love
Loretta

Another photo was of a man in a cowboy suit. Jesse read the words written in blue ink across the photo:

To Calvin — the star-maker
Your Pal,
Tex

"Is your dad a cowboy?" asked Mikey excitedly.

Jesse rolled her eyes. Veronica ignored the question.

"Don't touch anything!" exclaimed Veronica. She grabbed a small golden statue from Mikey's hands.

"I want to see it," whined Mikey.

"That's a Camera Award," said Veronica. "Dad'll be really mad if it gets broken."

"I won't break it, I promise." Mikey reached out for the trophy. But Veronica held it above his head.

Tears filled Mikey's eyes. "I want to see it!" he cried loudly. "Please?"

Veronica looked at Jesse and raised her eyebrows. Even though Veronica didn't say anything, Jesse could tell that she thought that her little brother was a pest. A *super* pest.

Jesse felt nervous. *It was just like Mikey to ruin things for her,* she thought. *Just when she was making friends with Veronica, Mikey had to mess it up.*

Jesse hurried to Mikey's side and bent down beside him. "Please, Mikey," she said. "Don't cry."

"I want to go home," announced Mikey. He sniffled, wiping his nose on the back of his jacket sleeve. "I want to go home right now."

Jesse sighed deeply. "But we haven't seen everything yet," she said. "Don't you want to see the album that has pictures of kids in it? They're kids who have been on television."

Suddenly Mikey's face brightened. "Movie star kids?" he asked.

Jesse nodded. Veronica lifted the big photo album from her father's desk. Then the three of them sat on the floor. Veronica opened the cover to the first picture, a young boy holding a plastic robot.

"I have one of those!" shouted Mikey.

Veronica turned the pages. Jesse looked at the pictures. She thought, *Gee! These kids don't look so special. I mean, they're not super beautiful. Maybe I have a chance. Maybe Mr. Peters will choose me to be in a commercial. Then he'll put MY picture in this album, too.*

The next photo showed a picture of an orange cat sitting by a bowl of food.

"Do you have any pictures with frogs in them?" asked Mikey.

"Are you serious?" Veronica asked, rolling her

eyes, then turning the page.

"Ha! Ha!" Mikey howled. "That girl has her underwear on! Ha! Ha!"

In the picture a young girl stood in front of a mirror in her underwear. The underwear was covered with a design of pink flowers.

"Hee! Hee!" Mikey giggled. "Is that what Jesse's going to do? Will she wear her underwear in the gym next week?"

As Veronica turned the page, Jesse's ears started to feel warm. As one photo followed another, Jesse found it hard to pay attention. At last she asked Veronica the question that was on her mind.

"Veronica," Jesse said. "Is your father going to do another underwear commercial?"

"I don't know," Veronica said, with a shake of her red, curly hair. "He might."

Mikey looked delighted. "Can I wear my Superman underwear?" he asked.

Three

JESSE spent almost every Saturday after-noon with Biff and Karen. On the Saturday before the screen tests, the three girls sat at the table in the Andrews' kitchen.

"I heard at school that the commercial is for ketchup!" said Biff.

Karen shook her head. "Susan Fredland said it was for breakfast cereal," she informed them. "Susan said that she heard Veronica talking to Patty about it. It's definitely breakfast cereal."

Jesse walked to the kitchen cupboard and pulled down a box of cereal. She carried it to the table. Biff took one look at the box and exclaimed, "Oh, gross! Toasty Crunchies! I hate that stuff! It tastes like cardboard."

"Dad won't buy cereal with sugar on it," explained Jesse apologetically. "This is all we have." She poured the cereal into a bowl. Biff stared at it and wrinkled her nose.

"Drown it in milk," said Karen. "Then it's not so bad."

"Then it tastes like *wet* cardboard," moaned Biff.

Jesse brought two more bowls to the table. "We'll take turns practicing," she said. "The only way we stand a chance at tryouts next Thursday is if we practice acting."

Biff looked at the bowl filled with little brown squares. "Why can't we do a commercial for chocolate cupcakes?" she asked.

"Or candy bars?" added Karen.

"*Pretend* you like it," said Jesse. "That's what acting's all about. I'll go first."

Biff and Karen moved back to watch as Jesse sat down at the table. She poured milk onto her cereal. Then she swirled a spoon around in her bowl. She loaded the spoon with brown squares and stuffed her mouth full. As she chewed, her eyes widened with delight. She smiled, too. But smiling with a mouthful of cereal caused a trickle of milk to leak from the corner of her mouth.

Biff and Karen laughed loudly. Jesse wiped the milk from her face.

"Okay, okay," Jesse said. "I'll smile *after* I

swallow the cereal. Let's start over."

Jesse put another spoonful of cereal in her mouth. She chewed it quickly and swallowed.

"Yum! Yum!" she said with enthusiasm. Grabbing the box, she read the name, "Toasty Crunchies! Golly! It's delicious! This is the *best* cereal I've ever tasted."

"Then it must be the *only* cereal she's ever tasted," whispered Biff. Karen couldn't stop giggling.

"Come on, you guys," said Jesse. "Get serious. We've got to be ready by next Thursday. The more we practice, the better we'll be."

"Can I eat some?" asked Mikey, walking into the kitchen. In his hands he carried a big, brown frog. "Mr. Bump wants some breakfast," he said. "Mr. Bump loves cereal."

"Don't bother us," Jesse said. "We're busy."

"Can I play with you?" Mikey asked. He set Mr. Bump on the table.

"Oooooo, gross!" squealed Karen. "The frog's next to the Toasty Crunchies!"

"Get him *off* the table!" shouted Jesse. "You know what Dad said about frogs in the kitchen."

Mikey grabbed Mr. Bump from the table. Then he quickly crawled under the table, with the frog in his hand.

"What are you doing?" moaned Jesse.

"I'm on the moon," said Mikey. "Me and Mr. Bump are ackernauts."

Jesse sighed. "He means *astronauts*," she explained to Biff and Karen.

"Me and Mr. Bump are ackernauts on the moon," repeated Mikey. "We live here all the time. Superman lives with us, too."

Jesse rolled her eyes. She breathed a deep sigh as she looked at her two friends. "I'm sorry," she said. "He's impossible."

"It's okay," Biff said. "I think he's funny."

"You're just saying that because you don't have any brothers or sisters," said Jesse. "Try living with a creep like Mikey for a while. You won't think he's so funny anymore."

Karen gave Jesse a sympathetic smile. "Believe me," she said. "My sister Kimmy's just as weird. Honest. I don't think Mikey's so bad. He's kind of cute."

Then Mikey's voice came from under the table. Jesse listened carefully to what he was saying.

"Hi, Superman, come on in. Mr. Bump and I are ackernauts. You can have some chocolate milk. Then will you please beat up my sister? She won't let me play with her. She yells at me and Mr. Bump. After you beat her up you can take me and Mr. Bump to the circus."

Jesse shook her head. Then she said to Biff and Karen, "Just ignore him. I'll practice this one more time. Then you guys can have a turn."

Jesse sat back down at the kitchen table. She scooted her chair closer to the cereal.

"Ow!" Mikey yelled. "You just squashed Superman."

Determined to ignore him, Jesse lifted her spoon. She stirred it around in the bowl. Her mouth puckered as she saw the Toasty Crunchies dissolve. The cereal and milk became a brown soup as her spoon stirred and squashed the soggy squares. It looked like the gravy her mother served with roast beef.

"Oh, gross!" exclaimed Jesse. "The crunchies aren't crunchy anymore!"

Jesse filled her spoon with brown mush. Slowly, she swallowed it. Then a grin spread across her face. "Yum!" she cried. "That's the best cereal I've ever had! It's delicious!" She held the box by her face and looked cheerfully at Karen and Biff. "Toasty Crunchies! Mmmmmm. I'll ask Mom to buy more." Jesse lifted a spoonful of dripping goo into the air. "Kids! Ask your mom to get you delicious Toasty Crunchies!"

Karen and Biff began to clap. "Yeah!" they cheered. "That was great, Jesse! Anyone who can eat that stuff should get an acting award."

Jesse bowed and then carried her bowl of Toasty Crunchies soup to the sink. She poured it down the drain. "Okay," she said. "It's Karen's turn."

Karen sat at the table in front of a new bowl. "Oops!" she said. "Sorry, Mikey." She turned to Jesse. "I think I just kicked your little brother," she said. "Sorry."

"It's okay," said Jesse.

Then the girls heard Mikey whispering:

"Mr. Bump and I are going to sneak up on my sister. We're going to turn the lights off and she'll be real scared. She'll be afraid that witches are under her bed. I'll get a monster to scare her."

Karen shrugged her shoulders. She poured herself half a bowl of Toasty Crunchies.

"If you want people to think you like the cereal, you need a big bowlful," suggested Jesse.

Karen stuck her tongue out at the thought of a whole bowl of brown squares. She tipped the box up and filled her bowl almost to the brim. Then she added milk. She leaned closer to the cereal and breathed in deeply.

"P.U.," she said. "This stuff stinks."

"I hope you don't say that at tryouts," said Jesse.

Karen sat up straight in her chair and began again. Holding her breath, she put a spoonful of the brown squares into her mouth. Then she chewed quickly. "Wow!" she squeaked. "This stuff is great! This is the best cereal I've ever had. I could eat a whole mountain of it!"

Karen took another spoonful and popped it into her mouth. Then she patted her stomach with her hand. "Mmmmmmmmmmm," she said.

"That was great!" exclaimed Jesse. "You really sound like you love it!"

Jesse and Biff applauded loudly. From under the table came the voice of Mikey saying, "This cereal stinks. I hate it! My frog hates it, too!"

Karen giggled. She left the table, and Biff took her place. Biff poured Toasty Crunchies into her bowl. Then she poured milk over it. She lifted the box and said, "Mmmmm. This is my favorite cereal. I just can't get enough of it." Biff ignored the spoon on the table. She lifted the entire bowl of cereal to her mouth. She tipped it up. She gulped it down as fast as she could.

Then suddenly Biff screamed. She jumped up from her chair, and the bowl of cereal sailed across the room. Toasty Crunchies rained down from above. Milk splashed onto the floor.

"He put the frog on me!" yelled Biff. "Your brother put that frog on my leg."

"Mikey!" yelled Jesse. "You come out of there right now!" Jesse reached under the table. She grabbed Mikey by the shirt and pulled him out. His eyes filled with tears. Clutching Mr. Bump, he began to cry.

"What's all the noise?" asked Mrs. Andrews. She came running into the kitchen. "Heavens! What happened?" She looked around at the mess. Mikey was lying on the floor with the frog on his stomach. Jesse stood glaring down at him, her hands on her hips. In all corners of the kitchen were little, soggy squares of Toasty Crunchies. Biff scrubbed her leg with a paper towel. "Gross!" she said. "I've got frog slime on my leg."

Mrs. Andrews looked sternly down at Mikey. "Did you put the frog on Biff's leg?" she asked.

Tears fell from Mikey's big brown eyes. "I had to," he explained. "Her leg was the elevator."

"The elevator?" asked Biff. "My leg was the elevator?"

Mikey nodded. He wiped his nose against his sleeve. Then he explained. "Mr. Bump was on the moon. He needed to go up the elevator so he could get in the rocket ship. Your leg was the elevator. The table is the rocket ship."

Suddenly, Biff began to laugh. "Gee!" she said. "I never thought of myself as being a frog elevator before. That's pretty funny."

Karen joined her in laughter. But Jesse just glared at her little brother. "Mom," Jesse asked. "Can't you do something? He ruins *everything*!"

Mrs. Andrews patted Jesse gently on the back. "He's just a little boy," she said. "He doesn't mean to be bad." Then she turned to Mikey. "Michael Vincent Andrews," she said. "No more frogs in the kitchen. I'm not going to tell you again."

Jesse took a paper towel and wiped milk up from the floor. "No more frogs in the kitchen," she muttered to herself. "Why can't I have a nice little brother? Why does my brother have to be such a creep?"

Four

THE sixth graders at Emory Elementary and Middle School had just one thing on their minds all week: screen tests for the television commercial. Thursday, the big day, finally arrived. When the bell ending the day rang, Jesse hurried to the elementary wing of the school. It was connected to the middle school by a long hallway. She stopped by the first grade classroom where Mikey waited for her. Jesse grabbed his hand and pulled him through the hall.

"Slow down!" yelled Mikey.

"I can't," replied Jesse. "It's time for tryouts. I don't want to be the last one there."

"Can I try out, too?" pleaded Mikey. "Please?"

Jesse looked down at her brother. She handed him a tissue. "Blow your nose," she said. "You're grossing me out."

As Mikey blew his nose, Jesse sighed. It was

sure tough to have Mikey tagging along with her every day. A month might not seem long to her mother, but to Jesse it seemed like forever!

Jesse walked into the gymnasium. Kids filled the bleachers, from the bottom row to the top. In the center of the gymnasium were bright lights on tall poles. The lights shone down onto a table. Beside the table stood a man with a mustache and little beard. Veronica ran over to stand by the man.

"That must be Mr. Peters," whispered Jesse.

"Hey, Jesse! We're up here!"

Jesse's eyes followed the sound of the voices. She saw Biff and Karen waving to her from the third row. Pulling Mikey behind her, Jesse climbed up. She and Mikey took a seat.

"Isn't this exciting?" asked Biff. "Look at the lights!"

"And look at the video camera!" exclaimed Karen. "It's just like a real commercial! I feel like a star already."

Jesse looked around her. The bleachers seemed to hum with excitement. Some of the boys were running combs through their hair. Girls were straightening their skirts. Several were putting on lip gloss and others were checking their faces in little mirrors.

"How do I look?" asked Jesse. "Does the bow look stupid?"

Biff and Karen noticed the red bow clipped above Jesse's ear.

"We like the bow," they agreed.

"Does my necklace look okay?" asked Karen. "Or should I take it off?"

Jesse and Biff carefully inspected Karen. "Leave it on," they said.

"Take it off," said Mikey. "It looks dumb."

"Mikey!" Jesse said sharply. "Don't listen to him," she said to Karen. "He doesn't know what he's talking about."

Mrs. Delwood, the school principal, walked to the middle of the gym. "Everyone!" she called. "I'd like your attention, please. We're ready to start the tryouts. You must all pay attention to Mr. Peters. Not everyone will be right for this commercial. And Mr. Peters needs only one child. Have fun, and good luck!"

Mrs. Delwood left the gym. Mr. Peters faced the crowd of students in the bleachers. Veronica stood beside him.

Jesse crossed her fingers and clenched her teeth. She made a silent wish to herself that her voice wouldn't squeak and her mouth wouldn't twitch with nervousness when it was her turn.

Mr. Peters held a piece of paper in his hand. "I have a list of everyone who signed up for tryouts," he began. "Today everyone gets twenty seconds on tape. That's all we have room for on this video tape. This is what we call a *screen test*. Later I'll look at the tape. Then I'll decide who will be in the commercial. Are there any questions?"

Paul Homer raised his hand. "What's the commercial about?" he asked.

Mr. Peters held up a big yellow can. "We're trying to sell grapefruit juice," he said. "Each of you will take a little sip of the juice. Then say a few words about how great it is. Okay?"

Jesse made a face. She whispered, "Yuck! I *hate* grapefruit juice. It tastes like ear wax."

"It can't be as bad as Toasty Crunchies," Biff whispered back.

Mr. Peters called the first name, "Allison Able!"

Jesse felt her stomach do a flip-flop. He was calling the names alphabetically by last name. Since hers was *Andrews,* that meant that she'd be one of the first to do her screen test. She took a deep breath and watched as Allison drank a paper cup full of juice.

"Mmmmmm! Yummy!" said Allison. She looked closely at the can. "Granny Smith's Grapefruit Juice is so good! And it's sweet, too. Just like me!"

The students in the bleachers laughed loudly. Mr. Peters smiled from behind the video camera. "Good," he said. "Very good."

Jesse thought to herself. *Oh, why didn't I think of saying that? I hope I can think of something funny.*

"Can we go home now?" asked Mikey. "I'm tired."

"Shhh!" hissed Jesse.

The next person to try out was Matthew Allen. He walked up to the table and took a cup of juice. He swallowed it in one gulp. Then he flexed his arm. "Wow!" he shouted. "This stuff tastes good! And it helps build muscles, too!"

The crowd laughed. Matthew continued talking. He said, "If I keep drinking this stuff I'll be the strongest guy at Emory. I'll be able to bust doors down with my bare hands. I'll be able to knock trees over! I'll be able to . . ."

Mr. Peters dropped his hand onto Matthew's

shoulder. Smiling, he said, "Your twenty seconds are up. Sorry. That's all we have time for."

Matthew flexed his arm once more. The Emory sixth graders laughed again. Then Matthew returned to his seat in the bleachers.

Jesse bit her bottom lip. She felt her heart pounding in her chest. She swallowed nervously.

"Jesse Andrews!" Mr. Peters called her name. For a moment Jesse didn't move. It was as if she were frozen to the bleacher seat.

"Go on," whispered Biff.

"You can do it," said Karen.

Slowly, Jesse rose to her feet. She climbed down to the gym floor. Jesse wondered if anyone noticed that her legs were shaking.

"Hurry!" urged Mr. Peters. "It's just twenty seconds per student."

Jesse walked faster. She stood by the table. The lights shining on her made her feel warm. Mr. Peters moved closer with the video camera. Jesse looked up and saw her reflection in the camera lens. She looked scared.

Mr. Peters glanced at his watch. He held a finger in the air. He counted quietly, "Five, four, three, two, one . . . go!" A small red light on the camera flashed.

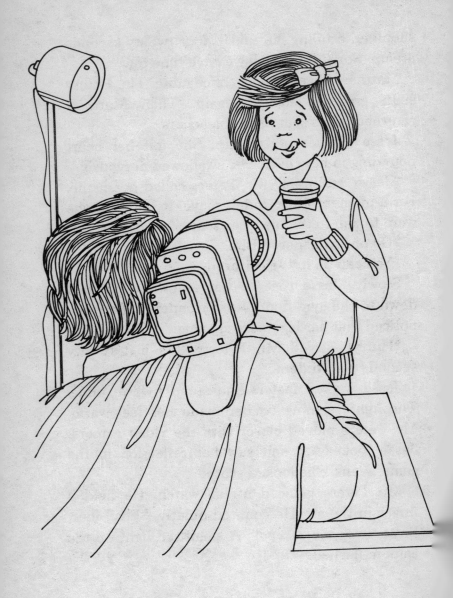

For a moment Jesse stood perfectly still. She reminded herself that this was the moment she had been waiting for—her big chance! The gymnasium was perfectly quiet. Jesse sprang into action.

Jesse picked up a paper cup from the table. She lifted the juice to her lips and drank it in one quick gulp. Then she ran her tongue over her lips. The warm, sour juice slid down her throat. "Wow!" she said. "That was great! Granny Smith's Grapefruit Juice is the best drink in the world! I love it!"

"My sister is telling a fib!" A small but insistent voice came floating down from the bleachers.

"Cut!" yelled Mr. Peters. "Who said that?"

"I did," admitted Mikey, waving from his seat between Karen and Biff. "Mommy told us never to tell fibs," he announced. "My sister Jesse just told a fib. She told me she *hates* grapefruit juice. She said it tastes like ear wax."

The bleachers erupted with laughter. Mr. Peters looked at Jesse. "Is that your brother?" he asked.

"Yes, unfortunately," sighed Jesse. "That's my brother."

Mr. Peters glanced at his watch. "We don't

have time for this," he said, impatiently. He looked at the list of names. "Rhoda Ashby!" he called.

Slowly, Jesse walked away from the camera and the lights. She couldn't remember when she had felt so disappointed. Mikey had ruined her big chance. Now, she'd never get to see Hollywood. And she'd never be a famous TV star. She'd never sign an autograph. No one would ever see her in a commercial. How could Mikey do it? *Why* did Mikey do it? Didn't he understand how much the tryouts meant to her?

Jesse found herself face to face with Veronica. "Boy, I really blew it, didn't I?" asked Jesse.

Veronica tossed her red curls. She patted Jesse on the shoulder. "It's your brother's fault," she said. "Not yours. If I were you I'd try to get rid of him. He's really awfully . . . awfully . . ."

"Creepy?" asked Jesse.

"Yeah, creepy," said Veronica. "If he were *my* brother, I wouldn't have anything to do with him."

Jesse climbed back into the bleachers. She took one look at Mikey and muttered, "The creep strikes again."

Five

JESSE watched as sixth graders gathered around Paul Homer in the school hall the following Monday.

"Congratulations, Paul!" someone was saying.

"Can I have your autograph?" someone else joked.

News traveled through the school quickly. Jesse stood by her locker and listened to the happy chatter in the hall. She was so disappointed she couldn't believe it! Mr. Peters had chosen Paul Homer to do the commercial.

"Hi, Jesse."

Jesse whirled around. It was Veronica. She looked as pretty as ever. Her red hair glistened with hints of gold. Her red and black dress looked like something out of a fashion magazine. She even wore black panty hose. Little golden hoops shone from her pierced ears.

"Hi, Veronica," Jesse said with disappointment in her voice.

"What's the matter?" Veronica asked.

Jesse sighed. "I don't mean to be a baby," she said. "It's just that I really wanted to do that commercial."

Veronica leaned closer and lowered her voice to a whisper. "I've got a great secret," she said. "You can be the first to know. But you have to promise not to tell anyone."

"A secret?" Jesse looked surprised.

"Promise not to tell?" Veronica asked.

"Sure," Jesse said. "I promise. Cross my heart." She made an *X* over her heart with her fingers.

"My dad's going to do *another* commercial!" Veronica whispered. "You'll get another chance. Screen tests are a week from this Thursday. That's just two weeks away."

"All right!" yelled Jesse. Then she clapped her hand over her mouth. "Sorry," she said. Her voice dropped to a whisper. "Can I tell Biff and Karen?" she asked.

Veronica lowered her eyebrows. "Don't tell anyone," she said. "Dad wants to announce it himself. He'd be mad if he knew I told someone.

46

Remember, you promised."

"Okay," Jesse said. "I promise. I won't say anything."

The bell rang and the hall buzzed with students racing toward their classrooms.

"Meet me after school!" said Veronica as she joined the rushing crowd. "Come over to my house. Okay?"

"Sure," Jesse agreed. She grabbed her books and ran toward class. She was the last person into the room. Hurrying down the aisle, Jesse dropped quickly into her seat.

Biff, who sat behind her, leaned forward. She whispered in Jesse's ear. "Did you hear about Paul Homer?"

"Yeah," Jesse whispered back.

Biff said quietly, "I guess we'll never be famous now. We'll never be in a television commercial."

"But maybe we . . ." Jesse caught herself just in time.

"Maybe we what?" Biff asked.

Jesse hesitated. "Maybe we . . . uh . . . uh . . . nothing." Jesse smiled nervously as Biff stared curiously at her.

Jesse pressed her lips tightly together, vowing

to herself not to break her promise to Veronica. But it made her feel funny. She'd always shared secrets with Biff and Karen, ever since kindergarten. They'd *never* kept anything from each other. Until now, that is.

Jesse was glad when Mrs. Stewart began calling the attendance. After that, the students opened their arithmetic books and Mrs. Stewart began multiplying fractions at the chalkboard. Jesse's mind wandered. She thought about the new tryouts. Maybe this time she'd be picked. *This* time she'd work extra hard to prepare before the big day. She thought to herself, *It sure is nice to have Veronica for a friend. Maybe she'll talk to her dad and ask him to choose me for the part!*

Jesse leaned her cheek into the palm of her hand, daydreaming of fame. She saw herself walking onto a stage. A rock band played in the background as Jesse stepped up to the microphone. The audience cheered and clapped. They threw flowers at her. She waved to her fans.

A sudden poke in the spine pulled Jesse back to reality. She noticed Mrs. Stewart staring at her. In fact, the whole class was staring at her.

"Thirty-six," whispered Biff ever so softly.

"Thirty-six."

Mrs. Stewart tapped a piece of chalk against the blackboard. "I'm waiting, Jesse," she said.

"Uh . . . uh . . . thirty-six," Jesse blurted.

Mrs. Stewart smiled. "That's correct," she said. "The answer is thirty-six." She wrote the number on the blackboard.

After school, Jesse hurried to her locker to get her coat. Biff and Karen were waiting for her. Biff pulled her mittens on. Karen's blond curls popped out from under her blue knit cap.

"Hurry," said Karen. "Mom said she'd make hot chocolate for us after school today. Can you and Mikey come over?"

"Oh . . . uh . . . ," Jesse said slowly. "I guess I forgot to tell you. I'm walking home with Veronica today."

Karen and Biff looked silently at Jesse. Then Karen said, "Gee. I wish she'd ask *us* to walk with her. I'd love to see the inside of her house. It's so pretty from the outside. The yard is giant!"

"Yeah. And her dad's famous," said Biff. "I'll bet Veronica knows lots of famous stars."

Jesse couldn't think of anything to say. She pulled on her jacket and shoved her hands into her pockets. "Well, bye," she said, then turned

49

and hurried down the hall.

She stopped by the first grade classroom where Mikey was waiting. "Come on," she said. "We're going to Veronica's house."

Mikey slipped his mittened hand into Jesse's. "Will she have anything for me to play with?" he asked.

"Maybe," said Jesse, as they started down the hall. They found Veronica waiting by the school's front door. At the sight of Mikey, a frown appeared on Veronica's face.

"Does *he* have to come?" Veronica asked. "I didn't know you were bringing your brother."

Jesse looked down at Mikey. He screwed up his face at Veronica.

"Sorry," said Jesse. "I'm stuck with him for a month." She thought about it for a moment. "Just three and a half more weeks to go," she added, trying to sound cheerful.

Mikey tugged at his sister's hand. "I'm going to be with you *forever!*" he said. "*And ever-and-ever-and-ever!*"

"No, you're not," Jesse said. She and Mikey walked with Veronica down the sidewalk. Winter's chill was in the air. A cold breeze scattered brown leaves across the street.

Mikey wiped his hands across his face. His cheeks were flushed and rosy. "My nose is cold," he complained.

Veronica looked down at him. "Maybe it wouldn't be so cold if you'd blow it," she said. "Gee! You're really grossing me out! Just look at you!"

Jesse looked up in surprise at the anger in Veronica's voice. A glance at Mikey's nose showed her that he needed to blow it. She handed him a tissue.

Jesse quickly changed the subject away from noses. "Will your father be home?" she asked Veronica.

"He might be," said Veronica. "He wanted to take some pictures for the new commercial he's doing."

"Tryouts are next Thursday?" asked Jesse, hopefully.

"That's right," said Veronica.

"Can I try out?" wheedled Mikey. "Can I be on TV?"

Veronica shook her head. "Nope," she said. "You're too young."

"I'm *always* too young," growled Mikey. "Mr. Bump is too young, too."

"Who's Mr. Bump?" asked Veronica.

Mikey pulled his hand away from Jesse's. He hopped down the sidewalk like a kangaroo. "Mr. Bump is a frog!" he shouted. "He hops like this. And he eats flies."

Jesse felt her ears grow warm as she noticed the frown on Veronica's face. Jesse explained, "Mr. Bump is Mikey's pet. Dad found him in Old Man Camber's Woods."

Mikey stopped jumping long enough to say, "There's ghosts, and witches, and monsters in the woods!"

Veronica wrinkled her nose. "A frog is a weird pet," she said. "I'd rather have a dog or a horse."

"Me, too," Jesse agreed. "I'd love to have a horse more than anything!"

"Frogs are the best!" yelled Mikey as he jumped backward and forward in front of the girls. Then his foot hit a rock and he tumbled down onto the sidewalk. "Ow!" he grunted. His notebook and lunch box clattered on the cement. Mikey moaned and rubbed his knee.

Veronica looked sternly down at him. "That's what you get for fooling around," she said. She turned to Jesse, saying, "Your brother is really a pain."

"I am not!" Mikey yelled, jumping up from the sidewalk.

Mikey behaved—sort of—during the rest of the walk to Veronica's house. To Jesse, it seemed to take forever! She kept waiting for Mikey to do something else to embarrass her.

When they reached Veronica's house, Veronica's eyes lit up. "Oh, good!" she exclaimed, pointing to the red sports car in the driveway. "There's Dad's car. He's home!"

"Will your dad put Jesse on television?" asked Mikey.

Jesse didn't say anything. But she was wondering the very same thing. Maybe now would be her big chance to impress Mr. Peters. Maybe he would think she was the perfect girl for the next TV commercial!

Six

JESSE didn't get to meet Mr. Peters at Veronica's house after all. He was in his darkroom developing film. A sign hung over the darkroom doorknob that said:

> DARKROOM IN USE
> DO NOT DISTURB

Jesse walked home with Veronica every day for the rest of the week. But by Friday she still hadn't caught sight of Mr. Peters. It seemed that he was always either in his darkroom or not home at all. Jesse shared her disappointment with Biff and Karen one morning as the three girls walked to school.

"Gosh!" she exclaimed. "I thought I would have met him by now!"

"Well, you and Veronica sure spend enough

time together," commented Biff.

"Yeah," agreed Karen. "We hardly ever get to see you anymore."

Jesse glanced away, feeling a little guilty. "Sorry, guys," she said. "Veronica's new. She doesn't know many people. I'm just trying to be friendly." Jesse stared down at the sidewalk.

"Want to go to a movie this Saturday?" asked Biff hopefully. "You can bring Veronica."

Jesse shifted her books uneasily in her arms. "Sorry, I can't," she said. "Veronica asked me over Saturday. I'm invited to eat supper and to stay all night at her house."

Karen and Biff looked at Jesse, then at each other. The three girls walked the rest of the way to school in silence, with Mikey trailing behind.

Jesse spent most of the weekend at Veronica's house. She had never stayed in a house so nice. Velvet curtains hung at the tall windows. Painted china vases stood upon fireplace mantels. Thick carpets covered the floors. It was a beautiful house!

The following Monday, the announcement was made to the sixth grade class about the second round of screen tests scheduled for Thursday. Excitement filled the air.

Jesse found herself spending even more time with Veronica. They waited for each other after classes, walked down the halls together, and stood at each other's lockers, talking between classes.

At lunch Monday, Jesse carried her tray through the school cafeteria with Veronica.

"Let's eat over here," Veronica suggested.

Jesse followed her to a nearby table. On the way there, voices called out:

"Hey, Veronica! The principal told us about the new tryouts. They're this Thursday?"

"Hi, Veronica. Tell your dad I'll be trying out again."

"Veronica! What's the new commercial going to be for? Is it for some kind of fruit juice again?"

"Hey, Peters! Put in a good word for me with your dad!"

It was cool to be hanging out with Veronica, Jesse thought. This is what it must be like to be a star. Everyone knows who you are. And everyone tries to get your attention. She was lucky to have been chosen as Veronica's friend.

In the distance she saw Biff and Karen sitting together. Lately, they never joined Jesse and Veronica for lunch. Jesse felt as if they were avoiding her. They never stopped by her locker anymore. She'd even caught them whispering together in class and thought that maybe they were talking about her. The only time the three girls got together anymore was on their morning walks to school. But even the walks weren't as much fun as they used to be.

Jesse knew that the reason she hadn't seen Karen and Biff after school lately was because she and Veronica walked home together every day. But still, was that any reason for them to ignore her at school? Was that any reason to quit calling her on the telephone?

Veronica leaned across the table toward Jesse. She cupped a hand to her mouth. "Listen!" she said. "Want to know a secret about the tryouts?"

Jesse dropped her sandwich onto her plate. "Sure!" she exclaimed. "Tell me!"

"You have to promise not to tell anyone," Veronica cautioned.

"I promise," Jesse vowed. "I kept your last secret, didn't I?"

Veronica nodded her head. "Okay. Here it is," she said, leaning closer. "I know what the commercial is going to be about." She paused, and a smile stretched across her face—the smile people

get when they know a really good secret.

"Well?" Jesse said. "Come on! What is it?" She looked carefully over her shoulder to make sure no one else was listening.

"Ice cream!" whispered Veronica.

"Ice cream?" Jesse thought it was too good to be true.

"French vanilla ice cream," Veronica said.

Just thinking about ice cream made Jesse lick her lips. "It'll be easy to say good stuff about ice cream," she said. "If I practice acting for the next three days then I'll be ready for Thursday's tryouts."

Veronica cocked her head to one side. "Practice acting?" she asked. "How do you do that?"

Jesse thought about it for a moment. Then she said, "I'll ask Mom to buy a box of ice cream. Then I'll eat it."

Veronica began to laugh.

"What's so funny?" Jesse asked.

"That's not how you practice acting," Veronica said. "I've met a million actresses, and that's not how they do it."

Jesse took the last bite of her sandwich. She washed it down with a gulp of milk. "Well, how, then? How do real actresses practice?" she asked.

"Dad has a book at home," Veronica said. "It's all about acting and voice lessons. He loans it to actors and actresses. It's got a bunch of autographs in it. Autographs from all the famous people who have borrowed his book."

"That sounds perfect," Jesse said. "Could I borrow it?"

"Sure," Veronica agreed. "Come over after school today. I'll get it for you then."

The bell rang, signaling the end of lunch period. During the rest of the day, Jesse found it hard to keep her mind on her classes. She couldn't believe how lucky she was! She was the only one in the whole sixth grade who knew that it would be an ice cream commercial. And she was the only one who would have *real* acting lessons from a book. *And* she was the only one who would have a book owned by Mr. Peters, himself!

This time things looked good. When Thursday came she'd be the best actress in the class! How could she miss?

That evening Jesse lay on her bed, flipping

through the pages of Mr. Peter's book, *Acting and Voice Lessons for Beginners*. There were autographs throughout in different kinds of handwriting. Jesse read:

> *Thanks for the book, Calvin. It helped me a lot. Love, Marilyn*
>
> *To a great director — with kisses from Shawna Eastman*
>
> *To my pal, Cal... from Gary B.*
>
> *Keep up the good work! Johnny Ventura*

Page after page was covered with autographs from stars. Jesse wondered if she might one day be asked to sign the book herself. She turned past the autographs to the text.

There were voice exercises to do, exercises that involved long words over and over. Some of the words didn't make any sense. And there were breathing exercises.

It seemed silly at first. But as Jesse read on, she learned that the exercises would make her voice sound better. The book said that every actress must have a good voice.

The sound of Mikey yelling out in the hall interrupted Jesse's reading.

"I can't find him!" Mikey hollered. "Mr. Bump escaped! He ran away!"

Jesse thought to herself, *If I belonged to Mikey I'd run away, too.*

Soon Jesse heard the sound of her mother's footsteps. Then her mother said, "Here he is, Mikey. He's under your bed."

"Hi, Mr. Bump," said Mikey. "You come on home now. You get back in your house."

Before Jesse knew it, her mother was calling from the dining room, "Gary! Mikey! Jesse! Dinner's ready!"

Jesse closed the book. With the help of this book, she would have the greatest acting voice in the sixth grade.

The delicious smells of fried chicken and gravy met Jesse as she joined her parents at the dinner table. "Yum!" she said. "Let's eat!"

"Wait for Mikey," Mrs. Andrews said. "Mikey! Dinner's ready!" she called.

Mikey came running to the table. "I had to wash my hands," he explained. "Mr. Bump got frog juice on me."

"Oh, gross," said Jesse under her breath. "Pass the rolls, please."

Mikey picked a roll out of the basket. Then he

handed it to Jesse.

"Yuk!" she said. "Don't touch my food. Why didn't you pass me the basket?"

Mikey frowned. "You said you wanted a roll," he said. "Didn't she, Mommy?"

Mr. and Mrs. Andrews smiled. "That's what you said, honey," agreed Mrs. Andrews. "He doesn't understand," she explained gently to Jesse. She turned back to Mikey. "From now on, Mikey, you pass the whole basket. You're not supposed to touch other people's food."

Mikey scooped a mound of potatoes onto his fork. Then he picked peas up with his fingers and pressed them into the potatoes. "Look!" he said. "I made a face!"

There was a pea for each eye. One for the nose. And three for the mouth.

"I'm going to eat it now," Mikey announced. He ate the potato-pea face and reached for his clown cup.

"Mom, isn't he too old for that cup?" Jesse asked.

"No, I'm not!" Mikey shouted. He set the cup on the table. His upper lip was covered with a white milk mustache.

Jesse sighed. She thought to herself that Mikey

would probably be drinking out of that same cup when he was in college. On the bottom of the inside was the face of a clown. Mikey loved to finish his milk to see that smiling clown at the bottom of the cup.

After dinner, Jesse and her father cleared the table. Mom rinsed the dishes and Jesse placed them in the dishwasher. She worked as fast as she could, because she couldn't wait to get back to the acting book.

When the last dish was in the dishwasher, Jesse ran back to her bedroom. She looked around.

"Hmmmmm. That's funny," she said. "I thought I left the book here on the bed."

But the book wasn't there. Jesse looked *on* the bed. Then she looked *under* the bed. Then she looked *behind* the bed, but the book was nowhere to be found. "Where can it be?" she wondered. Suddenly she knew. Under her breath, she muttered, "The creep strikes again."

Rushing from her room, Jesse yelled, "Mikey! Where are you?"

"I'm here!" he called. Jesse followed Mikey's voice to his bedroom. She threw open the door to find him playing with a toy train on the floor.

"Where's my book?" Jesse demanded.

"What?" Mikey turned his wide-open, brown eyes up to Jesse.

"What have you done with my book?" Jesse asked sternly.

Mikey seemed nervous. He looked guiltily away. "I needed it!" he said.

"Needed it? What do you mean?" Jesse stood above Mikey, with her hands on her hips.

Mikey pointed across the room. "Mr. Bump needed a new roof on his house," Mikey explained. "He kept jumping out. He kept escaping. I *had* to use it."

Jesse stalked over to Mr. Bump's cage. Sure enough, serving as a roof was the book, *Acting and Voice Lessons for Beginners*. It probably had frog juice all over it!

Jesse snatched the book up.

"Put it back!" yelled Mikey. "Quit tearing Mr. Bump's house up! Mom! Jesse's wrecking Mr. Bump's house!"

"You stay out of my room!" Jesse cried. "You and your stupid frog!"

"He's not stupid!" Mikey yelled. "Mr. Bump is the smartest frog in the world!"

Seven

JESSE, Biff, and Karen walked to school together as usual, but in complete silence. They just stared at the sidewalk. They didn't even talk about the screen test—and it was just two days away! Jesse thought it was weird that her old friends were becoming so strange.

Mikey ran along in front of them. He picked up a stick from under a tree and dragged it along the sidewalk. Then he yelled, "Look out! Monsters!"

Mikey jabbed at the air with his stick. He squealed and jumped backward. He whipped the stick around again. Then he kicked at the air with his foot.

Turning to the girls, he said, "Don't worry. I killed them."

Biff began to giggle. So did Karen. "Oh, Mikey," Jesse sighed. But for once she was glad that he was clowning around. It made them all laugh—something they hadn't done lately on their morning walks.

Biff smiled. "I think he's funny," she said. "Sometimes I wish I had a little brother."

"You can have Mikey," Jesse said. She held her books close.

A cold wind tossed Biff's long hair around. She hunched her shoulders up and shivered. "Hey, Jesse," she said. "Do you want to come over after school today? Mom said that we can play with her old makeup. She's got some neat stuff."

"Does she still have the eye shadow with silver glitter in it?" Karen asked.

"Yeah," said Biff, nodding. "We can make ourselves up like we're movie stars. Or rock stars."

"Or television stars," Karen said.

In spite of the cold weather, Jesse felt her ears turn warm. "Gee," she said. "I wish I could come. But I'm going over to Veronica's."

Mikey threw his stick into a yard. "Yuck!" he said. "I hate Veronica. She's a mean old witch."

"She is not!" Jesse exclaimed, glaring at Mikey. "Veronica's the prettiest girl in the sixth grade," she insisted. "She's the most interesting, too! She knows a lot of famous stars. And she used to live in Hollywood!"

Mikey just stuck out his tongue at Jesse and ran ahead. Biff and Karen glanced at each other. It felt to Jesse as if they were sharing a secret and leaving her out. The three girls walked the rest of the way to school in silence.

Mrs. Andrews wasn't home from work yet. Jesse glanced at the clock. It wouldn't be long now. She was always home by five o'clock. *Only two and a half more weeks of baby-sitting the creep,* Jesse thought with a sigh. Then everything would be back to normal, just like it used to be. Mom would already be there when Jesse got home from school.

Jesse finished her homework. Then she closed her bedroom door. Now was the time she had waited for all day. Opening Mr. Peter's book, she turned to the chapter called "Training Your Voice." She read the first exercise. It said:

Lie flat on your back. Relax. Breathe deeply. Put a book on your stomach and breathe deeply again. Watch the book rise and fall. This exercise will give power to your breathing.

Jesse found the biggest book she had, a dictionary. She lay on her bed. After breathing for a minute, she put the heavy book on her stomach. This time she breathed more quickly.

Jesse read Exercise #2. This exercise instructed her to breathe in quickly and yell, "Oh!" Jesse did this as fast as she could.

"Huh-OH!-huh-OH!-huh-OH!-huh-OH!"

With each breath, her chest rose and fell. *Gee,* she thought. *It sounds like I have the hiccups!*

As she repeated the voice exercise, she heard a knock at her door. "Come in," she said.

Mikey peeped around the corner. "Are you playing a game?" he asked. "Can I play, too?"

"I'm not playing," Jesse said importantly. "I'm doing voice exercises." She continued, "Huh-OH!-huh-OH!-huh-OH!"

"Hunko! Hunko!" Mikey yelled.

"Shhhh!" Jesse said. "You're mixing me up." She turned to the next voice exercise. This time, she marched in place like a soldier. Mikey began marching beside her. Jesse held the book and called out the words with each step. "No! Hey! Look out! Get out! Halt! March! Who goes there? Left! Right! Left! Right!"

Mikey marched beside her, stomping his feet

on the floor. He tried to say the same words that Jesse said. But he couldn't read them. And he couldn't remember them. So as he marched, he yelled, "Ouch! Bouch! Get out! Get out! Cooch! Cooch!"

Jesse stopped marching. "Mikey," she said. "Get out of my room. You're making too much noise."

"Cooch! Cooch! Bang! Bang!" shouted Mikey, still marching.

Jesse rolled her eyes. She knew that sometimes it was best to ignore Mikey. But it's hard to ignore someone in your bedroom who yells, "Cooch! Cooch!"

Mikey marched around the room. Jesse turned the page to the next exercise. It explained how to relax the jaw. The book said that relaxing the jaw would help to improve the voice.

Jesse followed the instructions, dropping her head forward, chin to chest. Then she moved her head from left to right and back again. She opened her mouth slightly.

"You look like Mr. Bojo," Mikey giggled.

Jesse scowled at him. Mr. Bojo was the oldest gorilla in the Emory Zoo. All the kids stood by his cage and laughed at him while he swung from tree branches. Mr. Bojo was the last thing in the world that Jesse wanted to look like.

Jesse returned to the book, determined to ignore Mikey. She repeated sounds that she read from the page: "Yah-yah-yah, yuh-yuh-yuh, yaw-yaw-yaw, yo-yo-yo."

Mikey ran around the room kicking up his heels. "Hee-haw, hee-haw, hee-haw, hee-haw!" he roared. "Look! I'm a donkey! Hee-haw, hee-haw!"

Jesse raised her voice to drown him out. "Fah-fah-fah!" she yelled.

"Hee-haw, hee-haw!" Mikey bellowed.

"Jesse! Mikey! What's all this noise?"

Jesse jumped at the sound of her mother's voice. She turned to see her mom standing in the doorway.

"It sounds like a zoo in here," her mother exclaimed. "I want you kids to settle down. What's going on in here, anyway?"

"Hee-haw," Mikey said.

"Michael Vincent Andrews. I'm not going to tell you again," Mrs. Andrews warned.

Jesse showed Mr. Peter's book to her mother. "See, Mom?" she said. "I'm practicing for the commercial tryouts on Thursday. But I can't get anything done with Mikey here. Would you please make him leave my room?"

A stubborn expression came over Mikey's face. He pushed his bottom lip over his top lip. "I want to stay," he said.

Mrs. Andrews took Mikey by the hand. She led him from the room, saying, "Your sister needs some privacy."

"Thanks, Mom," sighed Jesse. She closed the door behind them. Returning to the book, she flipped to a chapter on acting. This chapter explained how to relax before a big show. Jesse read Exercise #1.

Stand with feet slightly apart. With right hand draw a big number 1 in the air. Now do it with your left hand. Now do both together. Now draw a number 2. Repeat this up to number 9.

Jesse followed the directions, waving her hands in the air as she drew each giant, invisible number.

From just beyond her bedroom door she heard Mikey yell, "Mom! Come here! Jesse's trying to fly!"

"You creep!" Jesse yelled. She ran to her door and yanked it open. Mikey was crouched on the other side. Jesse slammed the door shut. Then she tore off a bit of tissue and stuffed it in the keyhole so he couldn't see in.

Jesse threw herself on her bed. Staring up at the ceiling, she wondered, *Can a six-year-old brother drive his twelve-year-old sister crazy?*

"Yes," she said, in answer to her own question. "Mikey's driving me crazy."

As she lay on her bed, Jesse remembered what Veronica had told her on the day when Mikey ruined the tryouts. Veronica had said, "If he were *my* brother, I wouldn't have anything to do with him."

It was pretty clear that Veronica didn't like Mikey. But with Mom working late, Jesse was stuck with him for a while longer. Would Veronica get mad at Mikey always tagging along? Would she decide to drop Jesse as a friend? Would she ask her father not to give Jesse the part?

"Gee," Jesse whispered to herself. "Tryouts are in two days. This is my last chance. Mikey better not ruin it again for me!"

Eight

IT was Thursday, the day of the screen test. Jesse dressed with extra care. She wore a blue pleated skirt and a matching blue sweater. She clipped a white lace bow onto the back of her head. Turning around in front of the mirror, she inspected herself. "You look great!" she whispered. "Maybe today you'll become an actress!" She hurried to the kitchen. As she ate her eggs and toast, she was careful not to get any on her outfit.

"Jesse, you're going to be late for school," warned Mr. Andrews. "You'd better get going." He carried the breakfast dishes to the sink.

Jesse peered out the kitchen window. "Biff and Karen aren't here yet," she said. "We always walk to school together." She looked puzzled. "I wonder why they didn't call? They always call when they're late."

"Where's Biff? Where's Karen?" asked Mikey. He squirmed while Mrs. Andrews buttoned his coat and buckled his boots.

"I guess they're not coming," said Jesse sadly. She opened the kitchen door and stared down the street. But there was no sign of Biff or Karen.

"Hmmm. That's strange," said Mrs. Andrews. "Karen and Biff are usually on time."

"They've been acting funny lately," said Jesse. She picked up her books and headed reluctantly for the door. It seemed strange to leave for school without Biff and Karen—even if they were barely speaking to each other anymore. Mrs. Andrews kissed Jesse and Mikey goodbye and hurried them out the door.

It hurt Jesse to think that Biff and Karen no longer wanted to walk to school with her. Were they jealous of her friendship with Veronica? *I bet that's it,* Jesse told herself. *They're mad because the prettiest, coolest girl in the sixth grade chose me to be her friend. That's it. They're just jealous.*

Then Jesse thought about the screen test. She, Jesse Andrews, was the only sixth grader in all of Emory School who knew that it would be an ice cream commercial. And she was the only student who had practiced acting from a real actors' book. Jesse quietly practiced a voice exercise as she walked along. She said, "Huh-OH!-huh-OH!-huh-OH!"

Mikey yelled, "Ho! Ho! Ho! Merry Christmas!"

Jesse glanced around, hoping no one had noticed. "Mikey, hush!" she said. "It's not even Christmas."

But Mikey kept yelling. It was embarrassing to walk down the street with a little boy who kept yelling, "Ho! Ho! Ho! Merry Christmas!" Jesse was glad when they reached school. She took Mikey to his first grade class. As she walked to her locker, she looked around for Biff and Karen. At last she spotted them, talking together by the water fountain. When they saw Jesse, they turned away from her.

Jesse was surprised at the way her old friends were acting. Then she tipped her chin up in the air. "If that's the way they want to act, then I don't care!" she said to herself. "Who needs them? I've got Veronica for a friend."

The bell rang. Jesse walked to her first class, arithmetic, and took her seat in front of Biff. Jesse ignored her. She sat straight in her chair and faced the front of the room. But it was weird to be sitting in front of someone who *used* to be her best friend. And it was strange that this ex-best friend wasn't speaking to her anymore.

Jesse was glad when arithmetic class was over. She left the room quickly.

The next class was art. Biff and Karen sat together in the back of the room. Jesse moved away from them and sat at a drawing board near Veronica.

Mrs. Bells, the art teacher, brought out a box full of paints. The box was filled with little jars. The colors were beautiful—blue, green, pink, purple, gold, gray, silver, red, yellow, and orange.

"Now, class," said Mrs. Bells. "We're going to learn how to use colors. We'll mix colors together. We'll discover how some colors look very nice next to each other. And other colors don't go together at all. Each of you can choose ten jars of paint and two paint brushes. You will keep your paint and brushes in a bag and bring them with you to class. Be sure to clean your brushes and take care of your paint. Okay?"

There was a rush for the paint box. Students grabbed their favorite colors. Jesse put her ten jars of paint into her art bag. Then she chose two brushes. Returning to her drawing board, she pulled on a large shirt to cover up her clothes. It would be awful to splash paint on her best skirt and sweater, especially today of all days. She had to look perfect for the screen test.

The rest of art class was fun. Jesse painted a green field full of rainbow-colored flowers.

"Very nice, Jesse," said Mrs. Bells. Jesse glanced over at Biff and Karen to see if they heard the compliment. But they didn't seem to. They were whispering to one another.

Jesse walked over to Veronica's drawing board. Veronica's picture was of a horse galloping in a circus ring.

"Are you ready for tryouts?" asked Veronica.

"I'm ready," said Jesse. She crossed her fingers.

Jesse spent the rest of the day trying to hide her nervousness. She didn't want anyone, especially Biff and Karen, to see how much the screen test meant to her.

The final bell of the day rang. Jesse's stomach did a flip-flop. She rushed to the bathroom and brushed her hair. The bathroom was full of other sixth grade girls.

"Oh, I hope Mr. Peters chooses me," said Gillian Davies. She fluffed her skirt.

"I hope it's not another grapefruit juice commercial," said Rosemary Jefferson. She wrinkled her nose.

Jesse put strawberry-flavored lip gloss on. She straightened the bow in her hair. Then she turned in front of the mirror.

"You look great, Jesse," Gillian said.

Jesse smiled. "Thanks," she said. "Oh, I'm so nervous!" She raced from the bathroom, got her coat, books, and art bag from her locker, and hurried down the hall. Mikey was waiting outside the first grade classroom.

"Where's Biff and Karen?" he asked.

Jesse's eyebrows lowered. "Who cares?" she asked. "Come on, Mikey. I've got another screen test."

"Goody!" exclaimed Mikey. "You're going to be in the movies again?"

"I never was in the movies," Jesse sighed.

They walked into the gymnasium. The bleachers were filled with excited sixth graders. "Come on," said Jesse. "I'll sit in the first row this time. I'm the third one in alphabetical order."

As they walked in, Mikey looked up. "Hi, Biff!" he called. "Hi, Karen!"

"Hi, Mikey," they called back. Jesse pretended

as if she hadn't heard. After all, they hadn't said hi to *her*.

The lights and cameras were set up in the middle of the gym floor. Mrs. Delwood, the principal, told the children to listen to Mr. Peters. He stood at a table with Veronica by his side.

"Today," he said. "We're doing an ice cream commercial."

"Yahoo!"

"Yeah!"

"Yum! Yum!"

Cheers rose from the bleachers. The students stomped their feet and clapped their hands. "Ice cream!" they yelled.

"Can I have some ice cream?" Mikey asked.

"Shhhh!" Jesse said.

Mr. Peters grinned apologetically. "Kids!" he said. "Calm down. I'm afraid I have some bad news for you."

The bleacher crowd became silent.

Mr. Peters continued. "The lights cause a lot of heat," he explained. "Because of the heat we can't use real ice cream. The lights would melt the ice cream. We have to use mashed potatoes instead.

The students groaned.

"Sorry," said Mr. Peters. "It's a trick of the trade. Scoops of mashed potatoes look like ice cream. We pour a little chocolate syrup over it. Then it looks just like the real thing on film."

"Potatoes and chocolate?" Jesse whispered. "Ooooo, gross!"

"Are you gonna eat them, Jesse?" Mikey asked.

"Yes," said Jesse, slowly.

"You'll eat them because you want to be on TV?" Mikey asked.

"I guess so," Jesse said.

Mr. Peters stood by the table. "We'll do it just like we did it last time," he said. "When you see the red light shining on the video camera, you begin. First you taste the fake ice cream. You hold up the box on the table. You read the name. And you say something great about the ice cream. Okay?"

"Okay," everyone agreed.

"Remember," said Mr. Peters. "You each get twenty seconds. That's all."

He read from the list of names. "Allison Able!"

Allison climbed down from the bleachers and walked to the table. The camera's red light blinked. Allison dipped a scoop of mashed potatoes onto a spoon. Streams of chocolate dribbled into the bowl. She put the chocolaty potatoes into her mouth. She smiled real big, and then she said, "Gross!" and spit the potatoes out into a napkin.

The kids in the bleachers began to laugh. But Jesse didn't laugh, because she knew her turn was coming up. And she wondered if she would be able to eat the crazy mixture herself!

Allison wiped her mouth with the back of her hand and ran from the gym.

Then Mr. Peters called out, "Matthew Allen!"

Matthew went to the table. He waited until the camera's red light shone. Then he shoveled a giant helping of potatoes onto his spoon. He swirled it around in the bowl to get extra chocolate on it. Then he stuffed it in his mouth. Matthew's eyes bulged as he swallowed the whole mess.

Matthew grinned. He picked up the ice cream box and read the label. "Polar Bear Ice Cream," he said. "Boy, is this good! I could eat a whole box by myself. I could even eat *two* boxes! This stuff is so good that I could eat it until my whole mouth froze! I bet it's good with chocolate sprinkles, too! I bet it would be good with peanut butter! I could eat Polar Bear Ice Cream with *anything*! I could even eat it in my sleep. Why, I bet I could . . ."

Mr. Peters pushed a button. The red light blinked off. "Your time's up, Matthew," said Mr. Peters.

"Darn," said Matthew. "I was just getting started." He walked back to the bleachers.

Mr. Peters read from the list. "Jesse Andrews," he called. "You're next."

Jesse turned nervously to Mikey. "Watch my stuff," she said. She laid her books and art bag on the bleacher beside Mikey. The little jars of paint rattled as Jesse stepped down. She whispered to Mikey, "Promise you won't say anything?"

"I promise," said Mikey.

"Miss Andrews, I have a schedule to keep." Mr. Peters tapped his foot against the floor.

Jesse ran to the table. The heat from the lights made her sweat. Mr. Peters poured chocolate syrup over a fresh bowl of mashed potatoes. It did look a lot like vanilla ice cream. Jesse waited for the red light on Mr. Peter's camera to flash. When it did, she daintily dipped a spoon into the fake ice cream. She chewed it, then said, "Yum."

Jesse took another larger spoonful. She swallowed it. Then she picked up the ice cream box. Looking straight into the camera, she said, "Polar Bear Ice Cream is so-o-o-o good! It's made from real cream, too."

Jesse was surprised at how relaxed she felt. She knew she looked great, too. She glanced out into the bleachers. Biff and Karen were watching her. Then she looked over at her little brother.

Before she could stop herself, Jesse yelled, "Mikey! Get out of my paints."

Mikey had removed several jars from the art bag. He had dabbed his finger into the jar of gold paint and was drawing a gold circle on his nose. A dribble of purple paint ran down his pant leg. Paint brushes clattered to the floor.

Jesse clapped a hand over her mouth. Mr. Peters yelled, "Cut!" The camera's red light quit flashing.

"Oh, Mikey," Jesse moaned. "You've done it again."

The crowd in the bleachers began to laugh and hoot.

"Mikey the monster!" someone yelled.

Mikey's eyes filled with tears. "I just want to see the colors," he said. "I want to finger paint."

Jesse ran to the bleachers. She saved her art bag from Mikey and put the lids back on the jars. Then she wiped paint from Mikey's pants with a tissue.

"Quiet, please," called Mr. Peters. "We've got to finish the other screen tests. Rhoda Ashby," he called.

Jesse gathered her coat, art bag, and books together. Then she led her little brother from the gym. Walking down the hall, she said through clenched teeth, "Thanks a lot, Mikey. That was my last chance. Thanks for ruining my life. Thank you very much."

Mikey looked up with his big brown eyes. He smiled shyly. Then taking his sister's hand in his, he said, "You're welcome."

Nine

A week passed after the ice cream screen tests and still there was no word from Mr. Peters. It was all Jesse could do to keep from asking Veronica about the tests. Jesse thought that Veronica might be tired of hearing about them, since that's all anyone in the sixth grade talked about these days.

Jesse sat across the table from Veronica in the cafeteria. She tried to concentrate on what Veronica was saying.

"My dad has done the most famous commercials," stated Veronica. She took a sip from her milk carton. Jesse chewed on a piece of pizza.

"Do you remember the commercial with the little puppies?" Veronica asked. "My dad did that one."

"Really?" Jesse was surprised. "I love that commercial!" she exclaimed. "It's so cute."

Veronica smiled calmly. "Have you seen the

commercial where the little boy sticks his elbow in the peanut butter jar? My dad did that one, too."

"Gee," said Jesse. "I knew he was famous. But I didn't know he was *that* famous." Jesse wiped tomato sauce from her mouth. She looked around the cafeteria. Biff and Karen were sitting together with another group of people. They laughed and talked. Biff turned to see Jesse staring at her. Embarrassed, Jesse quickly glanced away. Then she frowned. It looked as if her two ex-best friends didn't even miss her.

"Do you know the woman who does the White Roses Perfume commercial? She has blond hair and is really beautiful." Veronica was saying.

"The one where she's sitting in a garden?" Jesse asked.

"Yes, that's the one," said Veronica. "Her name's Marilyn. She had dinner with us one night."

"Wow!" Jesse exclaimed. "Did you get her autograph?"

Veronica nodded, her red curls bouncing softly. "Her autograph's in the acting book," she said. "Usually stars don't like people to ask for their autographs. You'd know that if you'd met as many stars as I have. But everyone who signed Dad's acting book is a friend of his who borrowed the book. That's why he has autographs."

"Oh," Jesse said. She took a big bite of her pizza. Pizza was her favorite food on the school cafeteria menu. But pizza was the last thing on her mind.

At last she couldn't stand it any longer. She just had to ask! "Has your dad said anything about the screen tests yet?" she blurted out. "It's been a week since he taped them. Has he decided who is the best?"

Veronica began to laugh. "I watched the tape with him last night," she said. "Your screen test was one of the worst ones."

Jesse felt her face flush pink. "I know," she moaned. "If it wasn't for Mikey I might have a chance at being an actress."

Veronica nodded. "He's pretty awful," she agreed. "I think he's the worst kid I've ever met. He's so . . . so . . . gross! I don't know how you can stand him."

"Sometimes I can't," Jesse admitted. "But I have only one more week to baby-sit him. Then Mom will be home again. And I won't be stuck with him after school."

The bell rang. Jesse and Veronica carried their trays to the kitchen window. Jesse found herself walking next to Biff as she left the cafeteria. Both girls ignored each other.

"Meet me after school?" Veronica asked.

"Sure," Jesse said.

Jesse went to Mikey's first grade class after school. "Look!" he said, holding up a drawing. "I did it by myself."

A scrawl of red and brown crayon covered the middle of the paper. There were holes where Mikey had scrubbed the paper too hard.

"What is it?" Jesse asked.

"It's a lion!" Mikey exclaimed. "He's eating a manimal."

"What's a *manimal*?" Jesse asked.

Mikey sighed, as if *everyone* should know what a manimal is. Then he explained. "A manimal is a big *cooch* with heads, and a tail, and it has thirty zillion teeth. And it jumps over the moon."

Jesse laughed in spite of herself. She looked more closely at the scribbles. "Hmmmm," she said. "Now that you mention it, it *does* look like a lion eating a manimal." She took Mikey by the hand. "Hurry," she said. "We're going over to Veronica's house."

Mikey dug his heels into the floor. Jesse tugged at his hand.

"I'm not going," said Mikey, stubbornly.

"Why not?" Jesse asked.

Mikey began to pout. "Veronica is a manimal," he said.

"Why do you say that?" Jesse asked.

"Mr. Bump said she was," Mikey explained. "Mr. Bump says Veronica is the biggest manimal in the world!"

Jesse felt herself losing her patience. "Veronica is not a manimal," she insisted. "There's no such thing as a manimal. There's no such thing as a cooch, either. And Mr. Bump can't talk." She pulled Mikey down the hall.

Veronica was in her usual place by the front door. "Hi, Jesse," she said. "Hi, Brat."

Mikey stuck his tongue out at her.

Veronica and Jesse walked side by side. Mikey lagged behind them.

"Hurry up, Mikey," Jesse said.

Suddenly a smile lit up Mikey's face. He ran up behind the girls. He yelled, "Beep! Beep! I'm a truck. Let me through!" He pushed his way between them. Veronica almost dropped her notebook.

"Why, you little . . ." she said angrily.

Mikey raced ahead. He made growling, rumbling noises. "Vrrrroooooooom, vrrrooooom!" he squealed. "I'm a truck!" He ran a zigzag down the sidewalk.

Jesse turned to Veronica with a smile. "If you ask me, the driver of that truck needs some driving lessons."

Veronica pursed her lips. Jesse saw that she didn't think that Mikey was at all funny.

"I'm sorry," Jesse apologized. "He's only six years old."

"Honk! Honk!" yelled Mikey. "Screeeeeech!" He pretended to turn a corner at top speed.

By the time they reached Veronica's house, Mikey had slowed to a walk. Veronica saw the red car in the driveway and said, "Dad's home!"

Jesse felt her heart jump. Maybe Mr. Peters would take one look at her and say, "You're the girl! You're the one we want for the ice cream commercial!" But then Jesse remembered her screen test. Veronica had told her that it was one of the *worst*.

Jesse and Mikey followed Veronica into the house. Veronica led them back to her father's study. She knocked on the door.

"Come in," said a deep voice.

Jesse crept into the room behind Veronica. It was dark. The curtains were drawn. Mr. Peters sat behind his desk, watching a video movie on a TV screen. Jesse turned to look at the screen. She was surprised to see Biff's face on the screen. Biff's eyes were opened wide, and she looked scared. Her voice trembled with nervousness. Her lips twitched. Biff held a box of Polar Bear Ice Cream. She said, "I'd walk a mile to eat this stuff!"

Mr. Peters turned off the screen with his remote control. He switched on his desk lamp. Scratching his beard, he looked at Veronica and Jesse. "These are all so bad," he said. "I can't use any of these."

"What's wrong with 'em?" asked Mikey, piping up in the background.

Mr. Peters thought for a moment. "The children are too afraid," he said. "They're not relaxed."

"I was *super* nervous," admitted Jesse. "The camera. The bright lights. Everyone watching me.

And some kids were laughing."

"Jesse almost wet her pants," Mikey said.

"I did not!" Jesse exclaimed. "You made that up."

Mikey picked up a trophy from Mr. Peter's desk. He turned it over and over. "This looks like a manimal," he said.

Mr. Peters seemed to be thinking. He ran a hand under his chin. Then he looked at Jesse. "You just might have something there," he said. "The lights. The camera. The crowd. All those things can be frightening to a child. Hmmmmmm."

Veronica snatched the trophy away from Mikey. She put it on a shelf out of his reach. Mikey crossed his eyes at her.

"I've got it!" Mr. Peters said excitedly. "I'll take a video camera around *to the children's homes*. We won't use the big studio lights. And there won't be a big crowd of people watching. It'll just be me and my little video camera. The children will be much more relaxed in their own homes."

"Good idea," Veronica said.

Mr. Peters nodded and snapped his fingers. "I don't know why I didn't think of it before," he said.

Jesse felt her heart begin to beat faster. Was it possible? Maybe she would have another chance! Maybe she would get to be in a commercial after all!

"There's just one problem," said Mr. Peters. "There's no way that I can go to the home of each child in the sixth grade class. I don't have time for that."

Jesse felt her hope fading. "How many screen tests will you do?" she asked.

"I'll do ten," Mr. Peters decided. "That should be enough."

"How will you choose who gets to do a screen test?" Jesse asked, nervously.

Veronica hurried to her father's side. She squeezed his arm and smiled up at him. "Can I help, Dad?" she asked. "I know all the kids in the sixth grade. I know who'll be the best. Can I help choose?"

Mr. Peters patted his daughter on the head. "Sure, kitten," he said. "You can help."

Jesse bit her bottom lip in excitement.

"I'm tired," Mikey complained. "I want to go home."

"Come on," Jesse said. "We better go. Mom will be home by now. Bye, Mr. Peters."

"Bye, Mr. Manimal," Mikey said.

Veronica, Jesse, and Mikey left the study. Standing on the front porch, Veronica said importantly, "Isn't it great? I get to help pick the kids who get to do a screen test. It'll be just like I'm a Hollywood big shot."

Mikey climbed onto the porch railing. He slid down to the yard below.

"Stop it!" yelped Veronica. "You'll break it!" She turned to Jesse. "Your little brother is such a creep!" she cried.

"I know," Jesse said sadly. "He's always been a creep. I guess he was probably born that way."

Jesse looked angrily at her brother. It would be just like him to ruin her chances again. The *last* thing she wanted was for Veronica to get mad at her because of her crummy little brother.

Veronica patted Jesse on the head. "Cheer up," she said. "Maybe you'll get another chance to have a screen test."

"Do you mean it?" cried Jesse. "I might be one of the ten?"

"Could be," said Veronica. "Just remember. *I* get to help Dad choose." She smiled mysteriously. Then she opened the door and disappeared inside.

Ten

ANOTHER Monday at school came to an end. Jesse leaned against her locker. She dropped her books to the floor. "I've been chosen?" she cried. "Me?"

"That's right," said Veronica. "I've already delivered Dad's letters to nine other kids. You're number ten." She smiled as she handed Jesse a piece of paper.

Jesse opened the letter and read:

> Mr. Calvin Peters
> Peters Advertising, Inc.
> Emory, Indiana

To: Jesse Andrews

You are among ten sixth grade students who have been chosen to give a screen test for the Polar Bear Ice Cream commercial.

Your screen test date and time have been scheduled for this Thursday, November 29, 8:00 P.M., at your home.

One child from among ten will be selected to act in the commercial.

Please have your parents confirm (by phone) the above date and time.

Sincerely,
Calvin Peters

Jesse threw the letter in the air and yelled, "Yippee!"

Other students came rushing over. "What's going on?" they asked.

"I get to do another screen test!" Jesse exclaimed. "This Thursday!"

"Me, too," called Don Edwards. He ran down the hall waving a letter in his hand. "I'm one of the ten!" he said. "Hollywood here I come!"

"I got a letter, too!" yelled Susan Fredland. She held on to the piece of paper as if it were made of gold. "Gosh! The screen test is in three days!"

One by one, the ten chosen sixth graders came forward with their letters. They slapped high fives in the air and congratulated one another.

"Just think, *one* of us will be on TV," Susan said.

Suddenly, they became quiet. Jesse looked at the others. They were all wondering the same thing. *Who would be the one person chosen to do the commercial?*

Don Edwards did a quick dance step. With a laugh, he said, "Don't worry about it."

That seemed like good advice. The ten students returned to their lockers. As she walked toward Veronica's locker, Jesse heard voices call out:

"Congratulations!"

"Way to go, Jesse!"

"Hope you like potatoes and chocolate!"

Jesse walked past Biff and Karen. Both girls turned their backs on Jesse. *Gee,* thought Jesse, *at least they could say something nice. I guess they're still jealous.*

"See? I told you I'd put in a good word for you," Veronica said. She stood by her locker, her silver earrings twinkling.

Jesse was so excited she hardly knew what to say. Her grin stretched from ear to ear. "Gee, thanks, Veronica," she said. "Want to come home with me? Maybe you could stay for dinner."

Veronica tipped her chin up in the air. "Is Mikey going to be there?" she asked.

"Well, yeah, of course," Jesse said. "I have to pick him up at his classroom."

Veronica screwed her mouth to one side. "No thanks," she said. "Your brother is really getting on my nerves."

"Uh-h-h . . . sorry," Jesse said, disappointed.

"I'll see you tomorrow," Veronica said. She wrapped a long, green scarf around her neck, pulled on matching gloves, and walked away.

At home, Jesse did her homework, while Mikey played in his room with Mr. Bump. Jesse heard the front door open and knew that her mother was home from work. A while later came clattering sounds and good smells from the kitchen, and Jesse could tell that her mother was cooking something delicious. Jesse hurried to the kitchen where she found her little brother already seated at the table.

"Can I lick the bowl?" Mikey asked.

Mrs. Andrews handed the bowl to Mikey.

"Can I have the beaters?" Jesse asked hungrily.

"Sure, honey," Mrs. Andrews said.

"Yum," Mikey said. "I love cookie dough."

Jesse smelled the aroma of cookies baking in the oven. She licked the beaters and thought to herself, *The kitchen is a nice warm place to be on a cold day.* Mrs. Andrews wiped her hands on her apron. "Jesse," she said. "I haven't seen much of Biff and Karen lately. Where have they been?"

"They had a big fight," Mikey said. "They're 'emenies.'" A glob of yellow dough clung to the tip of his nose. He pushed his tongue out as far as it would go and pulled the dough into his mouth.

Mrs. Andrews sat at the kitchen table next to Jesse. She looked deeply into her daughter's eyes. "Jesse," she said. "What's going on with you girls? Are you fighting? You've all been friends since kindergarten. It's a shame to lose friends like Biff and Karen."

Jesse leaned her chin into her hand. "Oh, Mom, they hate me," she moaned.

"Why would they hate you?" Mrs. Andrews asked.

"Because they're jealous of me and Veronica," Jesse replied.

"Is that what they told you?" Mrs. Andrews asked in surprise.

"Well, not exactly," Jesse admitted.

Mrs. Andrews spoke in her no-nonsense voice. "If you want to know why Biff and Karen are angry, why don't you ask them?" she said. "It's as simple as that."

Jesse stared blankly at her mother.

"Call them on the phone," her mom suggested. "Ask them to come over. You girls should talk about this."

Mikey had his face in the bowl. He licked every last speck of dough. From inside the bowl, his voice sounded like an echo. He said, "Jesse's too scared to call them. She's a fraidy cat."

"I am not!" Jesse insisted. She jumped up from the table and ran to the telephone.

Jesse could hardly believe that she'd called Biff, then Karen. It was funny to hear their voices after all the days of not speaking to one another. It was even more of a surprise to hear them say that they'd come right over. Jesse watched nervously from the living room window. At last, she saw her two ex-best friends walking up Robinwood Lane.

The doorbell rang. Jesse let Biff and Karen inside. For a moment the three girls stood silently staring at one another. Then Mrs. Andrews came into the hallway. "Why don't you girls go up to

Jesse's room? It's more private there."

Jesse led the way. The three girls sat on the bed together. They'd been there a thousand times before, but until today they'd always been laughing, or sharing secrets, or telling jokes.

At last Jesse spoke. "Why are you guys so mad at me?" she asked.

Biff and Karen looked at each other in surprise.

"We're mad at you?" they exclaimed.

Jesse nodded. "You never talk to me anymore. You don't stop by my house in the morning."

Karen stared at her shoes, then at her knees. Biff nervously wrapped a strand of her long hair around her finger.

"Come on, you guys," Jesse said. "I want to know what's going on."

Biff hesitated, then said, "You don't have time for your old friends anymore."

"That's right," Karen agreed. She nodded her curly blond head. "You're always with Veronica. You think Veronica's the prettiest girl in the sixth grade."

"And the most interesting," Biff said.

"And she knows movie stars," Karen added.

"And you'll do *anything* to be her friend," Biff

said accusingly. "You want to be on TV so bad that you'll dump your best friends."

Jesse felt her ears grow warm. She glanced in her mirror. Sure enough, her ears looked pinker than usual. It always happened when she was embarrassed.

"You wanted to be friends with Veronica so bad, that you forgot about us," Karen said sadly. "You quit walking home with us."

"You quit eating lunch with us," Biff added.

Jesse flopped back on her bed and stared up at the ceiling. "Gee!" she said. "I didn't know you guys felt this way. I just thought you were jealous."

"Jealous?" Biff laughed. "Jealous of Veronica? To tell you the truth, Jesse, I don't think Veronica is very nice."

"Me, neither," said a little voice from underneath the bed. "I think she's a manimal and a big cooch!"

"Mikey!" Jesse jumped up from her bed. Looking underneath, she saw her little brother lying among balls of dust on the hardwood floor. "You creep!" she yelled. Grabbing Mikey by the ankles, she pulled him into the center of the room. In his hands he held a big brown frog.

"Don't hit Mr. Bump!" Mikey pleaded.

"I'm not going to hit your dumb old frog," Jesse said. "Can't I have any privacy? You know you're not allowed in my room!"

Jesse felt her temper rising. She thought to herself, *Why do I have the creepiest little brother in the world? Everything Veronica says about him is true. He's the worst.*

Suddenly Biff began to giggle. Karen grinned so hard her cheeks dimpled.

"Look at him," Biff said.

Jesse looked. She saw a six-year-old boy, with big brown eyes, on his stomach on the floor. Clouds of dust clung to his hair and clothes. In his hands was a big, warty old frog.

Mr. Bump said, "Bawroooop!" He hopped straight up into the air. The girls shrieked.

Biff and Karen giggled so hard that the mattress shook. Then Jesse began to laugh, too. She couldn't help herself, Mikey looked so funny.

"I think he's cute," Karen said.

"I wish I had a little brother like Mikey," Biff said. "He can be a lot of fun."

"Do you really like him?" Jesse asked.

"Sure," Karen said. "He's pretty normal for a six-year-old kid."

"You mean all six year olds are weird?" Jesse asked with a grin.

"My sister, Kimmie, sure is weird," Karen said. "But mom says that all six year olds are silly. Sometimes I wish I could trade Kimmie in for a new sister."

"Are you still emenies?" Mikey asked.

"No, we're not *enemies*," Jesse said.

"Not us," said Biff. "We've been friends forever!"

"And we'll go on being friends forever," Karen added.

Jesse felt great. She said, "I'm sorry I spent so much time with Veronica. I didn't mean to ignore you guys. Let's start walking to school again. And eating lunch together, okay?"

"Okay," Biff said. "Oh, by the way, congratulations on being chosen for the screen test. I hope you get it."

"Yeah, good luck," Karen said.

Jesse crossed her fingers. "I'm so excited," she said. "Mr. Peters is coming this Thursday. In just three days I might be a TV star!"

Eleven

"HI, Biff. Hi, Karen!" Mikey yelled as Jesse, Biff, and Karen stopped by the first grade room after school. Jesse helped Mikey pull on his mittens. The three girls walked home with Mikey trailing behind them. Even though it was a cold day, the sun shone brightly.

"Where's Veronica?" Biff asked.

"Her father picked her up early today," Jesse explained. "She had a dentist appointment."

Mikey found a small rock to kick. "This is a football," he said. "And I'm the star quarterback. I'm the best quarterback in the world."

"He's more like a *nickel*-back," Jesse joked. The girls laughed.

"Is your mom still working late?" Biff asked.

"Yeah," Jesse answered. "But this is the last week. Next week I won't have to baby-sit Mikey anymore. Maybe we can go to the roller rink after

111

school one day."

"Great!" said Karen. "I'll get my mom to drive us."

"Can I come?" Mikey asked. He pushed his way in between Jesse and Biff. "Please?" he pleaded.

"Next week you're going to stay home with Mom," Jesse said.

"You cooch!" cried Mikey. He frowned and kicked his rock out into the street.

"What's a *cooch*?" asked Biff.

"Don't ask me," Jesse said with a sigh.

The phone was ringing as Jesse and Mikey walked in the front door. Jesse ran to the kitchen to answer it. "Hello?" she said.

"Hi, Jesse. It's Veronica. Are you ready for the screen test tomorrow?"

"You bet I am," Jesse exclaimed. "I can't wait!"

"Can you come over?" Veronica asked. "I'll show you some more of my dad's photo albums."

"Sure," said Jesse. "I'll be right over. It'll just be a few minutes. First I've got to help Mikey change out of his school clothes."

There was silence on the other end. Veronica sighed deeply. "Jesse," she said at last. "Would

you please not bring your brother? You know how he is. He's such a brat."

Jesse felt her stomach do a somersault. "I *have* to bring him," she explained. "I can't leave him alone here. He's too young. He's my responsibility while Mom's at work."

Veronica didn't say a thing.

"This is the last week," Jesse hurried to say. "I won't have to baby-sit him anymore after this week."

"Don't you want to be my friend? Remember who got you picked for the screen test. I could get you un-picked, you know. Don't you want to do the screen test?" Veronica asked.

"Sure I do!" Jesse said.

"Well, then come over to my house," Veronica said. "And *don't bring your brother.*"

Jesse couldn't believe what she was hearing. Didn't Veronica understand that a six year old can't be left alone?

"Gosh, Veronica," said Jesse. "I *can't* leave Mikey here. I can come over when Mom gets home. Is that okay?"

"Choose," Veronica ordered. "I'm tired of always getting stuck with Mikey. It's me or him!"

Just then the kitchen door opened. Jesse

jumped at the sound.

"Hi, honey," said Mrs. Andrews. She unbuttoned her coat and then stamped her feet to get them warm. "Who's on the phone?" she asked.

"Veronica," Jesse whispered.

"What's wrong?" Mrs. Andrews asked. "You look like you saw a ghost."

"Jesse? Jesse?" It was Veronica's voice again. She said, "Is that your mother I hear? Great! Now you can come over. See you in a few minutes?"

Jesse's voice was almost shaking as she said, "Sorry, Veronica. I made my choice. I choose my brother." With that, Jesse hung up the telephone. Her eyes welled with tears. Her chin trembled.

"Jesse! What's wrong?" her mother asked.

Jesse sighed deeply. "Now I won't get to do the screen test," she said. "Veronica's going to tell her dad to get someone to take my place."

"Are you sure?" Mrs. Andrews asked. She lay her hand gently on Jesse's shoulder.

"I'm sure," Jesse said. "Forget the screen test. I'll never get another chance." Tears of disappointment ran down her cheeks. Her mother hugged her close. Jesse wondered if the tears would ever stop.

Twelve

JESSE tried to talk to Veronica at school the next day. And she tried the day after that. But Veronica always seemed to be surrounded by a group of admiring kids. As Jesse walked by the group she heard Paula Kurtz say, "Really, Veronica? Your dad said I could have a screen test, too?"

Jesse knew then that Paula had been chosen to take her place. She saw Paula and Veronica eat lunch together in the cafeteria. And she saw them walk away together after school.

Jesse did her homework that Thursday evening. Then she sat in front of her mirror and looked at herself. "Your nose is too big, anyway," she said sadly. "And your chin is too pointy. You could never be an actress." She looked down at her clothes—sweatpants, an old T-shirt, running shoes with holes in the toes. She didn't look anything like the cute kids in Mr. Peters's photo albums. "Gee," said Jesse. "Who was I kidding? Why would anyone want me to be in a commercial?"

"Why did I do it?" Jesse asked herself. "Why did I blow my one chance? Why did I fight with Veronica?" She thought about it for a minute. Then she answered herself. "I did it for my brother," she admitted. "For my little, creepy brother," she added, which did sound a little funny. But she really didn't feel like smiling, so she threw herself onto her bed and buried her face in her pillow.

From under the pillow, Jesse heard a knock at the door. "Who is it?" Jesse called.

Mrs. Andrews stuck her head into Jesse's room. "There's someone here to see you," she said, smiling.

Jesse followed her mother into the living room. Her mouth opened with surprise when she saw Mr. Peters. He held a video camera in one hand, and a box of Polar Bear Ice Cream in the other.

"Hello, Jesse," he said, cheerily. "Are you ready for your screen test?"

Jesse looked down at her baggy sweatpants and faded T-shirt.

"I'm on a tight schedule," Mr. Peters said. "Let's start taping."

"B-b-b-but," stammered Jesse. "I thought you weren't . . ."

Jesse's father led Mr. Peters into the kitchen. "Come on, Stardoodle," her father called. "Now's your big chance!"

Mikey ran into the kitchen. He held Mr. Bump in his hands. "Can we be in the commercial?" he pleaded.

Mr. Andrews pulled Mikey out of the way. Jesse felt her heart begin to flutter. *I look awful,* she thought. *But this is my big chance. I'll do my best!*

Jesse sat at the kitchen table. Mr. Peters put the box of ice cream on the table.

"You mean it's not mashed potatoes?" asked Jesse.

"Nope. We've got the real thing this time," said Mr. Peters with a smile. "Without the studio lights it doesn't get so hot. The ice cream won't melt."

Jesse looked more closely at the box. "Chocolate chip?" she asked hopefully.

"That's right!" Mr. Peters said. "Let's get started. Shall we?"

Mrs. Andrews put a bowl and a spoon on the table. "Can we watch?" she asked.

"Sure," Mr. Peters said. "Stand back there. Right. I'll videotape from over here." He walked to the other side of the table, facing Jesse.

Everything seemed to be happening so fast! Jesse could hardly believe that Mr. Peters—TV producer—was in her house. And he was going to make a commercial of her!

"Same thing as last time," Mr. Peters said. "Be natural. Taste the ice cream. Say whatever comes into your head." He stepped backward. Jesse watched as Mr. Peters held the video camera up to his face. A whirring noise began when he pushed a button. The red light flashed on. "Roll 'em!" he said.

Jesse opened the box of Polar Bear Ice Cream. She dug her spoon into the rich, creamy stuff. Then she spooned it into her bowl. Little chips spotted the smooth white treat. She dipped her spoon in and took a mouthful.

"Mmmmmmm," she said. "This is really good." She took another taste. "It's creamy. And the chips are extra chocolaty. I like the way they melt after the ice cream melts." Jesse laughed. *This is great!* she thought. *All I have to do is eat this ice cream. This is easy!*

"Can I have some?" Mikey yelled. He ran to the table and looked longingly into Jesse's bowl of ice cream. Mr. Andrews started after him, but Mr. Peters motioned him back.

"Mikey!" Jesse yelled. Then she shrugged her shoulders. "I guess I can't blame him," she said, looking at Mr. Peters. "It's pretty hard to watch someone else eat ice cream. Especially when it's so good!"

Mikey placed Mr. Bump on the table. Then he reached for Jesse's spoon. Shoveling a big spoonful of ice cream into his mouth, he said, "Mif ifiwy goooooo."

Jesse laughed. "I think he said, 'This is really good,' " she translated.

Mikey dug his spoon into the ice cream once more. He pulled out a heap of white ice cream loaded with little brown chips. Then he offered the spoonful to Mr. Bump.

"Mr. Bump wants some, too," he said.

"What?" Jesse began to giggle. "How do you know your frog wants ice cream?" she asked.

"Because he thinks the chocolate chips are flies!" Mikey said.

"Oooooo, gross!" Jesse squealed.

Mikey held the ice cream in front of Mr. Bump's face. Mr. Bump's throat swelled in and out. His bulging eyes blinked. Then he jumped.

Jesse caught him just before he fell off the table.

"Cut!" Mr. Peters yelled.

Jesse was having so much fun, she'd almost forgotten the camera was on. "I'm sorry," she said. "I guess Mikey just has to get into everything."

Mr. Andrews hurried forward. "If you like, we can take Mikey into the other room. You can do the taping over again."

"No," said Mr. Peters. "This is just what I wanted! The children were natural! They were delightful! Charming! I'll edit this tape and transfer it to one-inch video tape. Then it'll be ready for distribution to TV stations."

"You mean it?" Jesse cried. "Mikey didn't ruin it?"

Mr. Peters put the camera back into its case. "This is the best screen test I've done," he said. "Having a brother and sister together is what makes it work!"

"A brother, a sister, and a frog," Mikey said. "Don't forget Mr. Bump."

Thirteen

"**H**URRY! Turn it on!" Jesse yelled. She ran to the couch with a bowl of popcorn. Mikey was right behind her carrying Mr. Bump. Mr. Andrews turned on the television set.

"Is it on yet?" called Mrs. Andrews from the kitchen.

"Hurry, Mom!" Jesse shouted.

Biff and Karen sat on the couch next to Jesse. "I can't believe we finally get to see it," Biff said. "We've waited months."

Jesse sighed. "Mr. Peters said that's how it is in the TV business," she knowingly explained. "It takes a while before the commercial makes it to TV."

Mrs. Andrews placed a bowl of cheese dip, a

plate of crackers, and a stack of paper plates on the coffee table. She sat down in a chair.

"Here it is!" Mikey screamed.

Everyone was quiet as the commercial came on.

"There's our kitchen," Mikey yelled.

"Shhhh!" Jesse hissed.

The commercial began. Jesse watched herself tasting the ice cream. When her voice began, Jesse said, "Do I really sound like that?" She whispered to Karen, "I can't believe I wore that awful T-shirt!"

Jesse leaned closer to the TV. She saw Mikey come bounding into the picture.

"There's me with Mr. Bump!" Mikey shrieked. "Look, Mr. Bump! You're a star!" He held the frog up so that he could see the TV better.

The commercial ended. "That was fast," Jesse said.

Mr. Andrews turned the TV off. He said with a wink, "My kids are famous now."

"Oh, Dad," Jesse said, feeling her ears turn warm.

Biff began to laugh. "Can I have your autograph?" she asked jokingly. She handed Jesse the stack of paper plates and a pen.

Jesse signed her full name:

To Biff
from your famous friend
Jessica Marie Andrews

Then Jesse signed another plate for Karen. She wrote:

To Karen
from your beautiful, rich friend
Jessica Marie Andrews

Biff and Karen read the plates and moaned, "Oh, give us a break!"

Biff put crackers and a scoop of cheese dip onto her plate.

"Hey!" Jesse laughed. "That's no way to treat my autograph."

From the corner of Jesse's eye, she saw a brown frog leaping high into the air.

"Aaawwwrrrg!" she screamed. She watched as Mr. Bump landed right in the middle of the cheese dip. Then he jumped again. He went straight up into the air. This time he landed in Jesse's lap on her paper plate.

Mr. Andrews reached out and caught the runaway frog. "Hey, Winkypopper," he said. "I think it's time for Mr. Bump to go back into his house. I don't know what this frog may be up to."

Mikey jumped and pointed at the paper plate in Jesse's lap. "Look!" he cried. "Mr. Bump gave Jesse his autograph!"

Jesse looked. There was a cheesy, orange footprint of a frog on her plate. "Look!" she exclaimed. "It's the autograph of the most famous frog in Emory, Indiana."

Jesse reached out and squeezed her little brother's hand. She said, "You know, you're not too bad . . . for a creep."

Mikey grinned back at his sister. "You're not too bad either," he said, "for a *cooch!*"

About the Author

"I remember what it was like to be a kid," says JANET ADELE BLOSS. "I understand how kids feel things very deeply. And I know that kids love to laugh."

Anyone who reads Janet's book will agree that she has a keen insight into the emotional lives of children. The characters in her books live in a kids' world of pesty sisters, creepy brothers, runaway pets, school bullies, and good friends.

The characters laugh, cry, dream, and race through the pages of her stories. As one reader says: *"When I read your books, it's like I'm watching a movie."*

Janet showed signs of becoming an author as early as third grade when she wrote a story entitled *Monkeys on the Moon.* By the time Janet reached fifth grade she had decided to become an author. She also wanted to be a flamenco dancer, a spy, a skater for roller derby, and a beach bum in California. But fortunately for her readers it was the dream of becoming an author that came true.

"I've always loved books and children," says Janet. "So writing for children is the perfect job for me. It's fun."

Although Janet's first love is writing, her other interests include dancing, music, camping, swimming, ice-skating, and cats.